THE RISING FORCE

The epic begins . . .

STAR WARS
EPISODE I
THE PHANTOM MENACE™
By Patricia C. Wrede
Based on the screenplay and story by George Lucas

See Episode I through their eyes . . .

STAR WARS
EPISODE I
JOURNAL

Anakin Skywalker
Queen Amidala

. . . and more to come

Before there was *The Phantom Menace*, there was . . .

STAR WARS

JEDI APPRENTICE

#1 The Rising Force

#2 The Dark Rival

. . . and more to come

STAR WARS

JEDI APPRENTICE

The Rising Force

Dave Wolverton

LUCAS BOOKS

SCHOLASTIC INC.

New York Toronto London Auckland Sydney
Mexico City New Delhi Hong Kong

Cover design by Madalina Stefan. Cover art by Cliff Nielson.

Scholastic Children's Books
Commonwealth House, 1-19 New Oxford Street, London WC1A 1NU
a division of Scholastic Ltd
London — New York — Toronto — Sydney — Auckland
Mexico City — New Delhi — Hong Kong

Published in the UK by Scholastic Ltd, 1999
Published in the USA by Scholastic Inc., 1999

ISBN 0 439 01286 4

1 3 5 7 9 10 8 6 4 2

Printed in the U.S.A.

CHAPTER 1

The blade of the lightsaber hissed through the air. Obi-Wan Kenobi could not see its red gleam through the blindfold pressing on his eyes. He used the Force to know precisely when to duck.

The searing heat of his opponent's lightsaber blade slashed overhead, nearly burning him. The air smelled like lightning.

"Good!" Yoda called from the sidelines of the room. "Let go. Let your feelings guide you."

The words of encouragement spurred Obi-Wan on. Because he was tall and strong for a twelve-year-old, many assumed that he'd have the advantage in battle.

But strength and size counted for nothing where agility and speed were needed. Nor did they have any effect on the Force that he had not yet mastered.

Obi-Wan listened intently for the sound of his

foe's lightsaber, for his breathing, for the scrape of a shoe against the floor. Such sounds echoed loudly in the small, high-ceilinged chamber.

A random jumble of blocks on the floor added another element to the exercise. He had to use the Force to sense those, too. With such uneven ground, it was easy to lose his footing.

Behind Obi-Wan, Yoda warned, "Keep your guard up."

Obi-Wan obediently raised his weapon and rolled to his right as his opponent's blade slammed down into the floor beside him. He took a small leap back, clearing a pile of blocks. Obi-Wan heard the sing of the lightsaber as his foe attempted a hasty strike motivated by irritation and fatigue. Good.

Sweat trickled underneath the blindfold, making his eyes sting. Obi-Wan blocked it out, along with his pleasure at his opponent's clumsiness. He could imagine himself a full Jedi Knight, battling a space pirate . . . a Togorian with fangs as long as Obi-Wan's fingers. In his mind, Obi-Wan saw the armored creature glare at him through eyes that were mere green slits. Its claws could easily shred a Human.

The vision energized him, helped him let go of his fears. In seconds, his every muscle was tuned to the Force. It moved through him, giving him the agility and speed that he needed.

Obi-Wan swung his blade up to block the next blow. The attacker's lightsaber hummed and whirled down. Obi-Wan leaped high, somersaulting over his attacker's head, and thrust his lightsaber down where the Togorian's heart would be.

"Aargh!" The other student howled in surprised rage as Obi-Wan's hot blade struck his neck. If Obi-Wan had been using a Jedi Knight's lightsaber, it would have been a killing blow. But apprentices in the Jedi Temple used training sabers set at low power. The touch of the blade only gave a searing kiss, one that the healers might need to tend.

"That was a lucky blow!" the wounded apprentice shouted.

Until that moment, Obi-Wan had not known who he was fighting. He'd been led into the room blindfolded. Now he recognized the voice: Bruck Chun. Like Obi-Wan, Bruck was one of the oldest apprentices in the Jedi Temple. Like Obi-Wan, Bruck hoped to be a Jedi Knight.

"Bruck," Yoda called calmly. "Leave your blindfold on. A Jedi needs not his eyes to see."

But Obi-Wan heard the boy's blindfold slap to the ground. Bruck's voice was choked with fury. "You clumsy oaf!"

"Calm yourself, you will!" Yoda warned Bruck in a sharp tone he rarely used.

Every student at the Jedi Temple had his or her weaknesses. Obi-Wan knew his own too well. Every day, he had to struggle to control his anger and his fear. The Temple was a test of character as much as skill.

Bruck struggled with his own simmering anger that could quickly ignite into hot rage. He usually kept it well under control, so that only other initiates had glimpsed it.

Bruck also held grudges. A year ago, Obi-Wan had stumbled in a Temple corridor, tripping Bruck, who had fallen. It had been an accident, caused by legs and feet that were growing too fast on both boys, but Bruck felt sure that Obi-Wan had done it on purpose. Bruck's dignity was very important to him. The laughter of the other students had goaded him. He'd called Obi-Wan an oaf then — *Oafy*-Wan.

The name had stuck.

The worst thing was that it was true. Often, Obi-Wan felt that his body was growing too fast. He couldn't seem to catch up with his long legs and large feet. A Jedi should feel comfortable in his body, but Obi-Wan felt awkward. Only when the Force was moving through him did he feel graceful or sure.

"Come on, Oafy," Bruck taunted. "See if you can hit me again! One last time, before they throw you out of the Temple!"

"Bruck, enough!" Yoda said. "Learn to lose as well as win, a Jedi must. Go to your room, you will."

Obi-Wan tried not to feel the sting of Bruck's words. In four weeks he'd turn thirteen and would have to leave the Temple. Taunts like Bruck's were becoming more and more frequent as his birthday drew nearer. If he did not become a Padawan within the next four weeks, he'd be too old. He'd been listening for rumors intently, and had found that no Jedi was scheduled to come in search of a Padawan before it was too late. He was afraid that he'd never become a Jedi Knight. That fear angered him. Enough for him to make a foolish boast.

"You don't have to send him away, Master Yoda," he said. "I'm not afraid to fight *him* without his blindfold."

Color blazed in Bruck's cheeks, and his ice-blue eyes narrowed. Yoda merely nodded, taking in Obi-Wan's words. The truth was that Obi-Wan was just as exhausted as Bruck. He hoped Yoda would send both of them to their rooms instead of allowing them to fight again.

After a long moment, however, Yoda said, "All right. Continue. Much to learn, you have. Use the blindfolds, you must."

Obi-Wan turned and bowed to Yoda, accepting the order. He knew that Yoda was fully aware of his fatigue. Although he wished that the Master would grant him a reprieve, he accepted the wisdom of all of Yoda's decisions, great and small.

Obi-Wan tightened his blindfold. He pushed away his fatigue, willed his muscles to obey. He tried to forget that he was fighting Bruck, or that his chance to become a Jedi Knight was almost past. He concentrated instead on the image of the Togorian pirate, its orange-striped fur covered by black armor.

Obi-Wan could sense the Force flowing around him, within him. He could feel the living Force in Bruck, the dark ripples caused by Bruck's anger. His impulse was to match that anger with his own. He had to resist it.

Obi-Wan assumed a defensive stance as Bruck lunged. He let the Force guide him as it had done earlier. He blocked the next blow easily. Then he jumped high to avoid another blow and landed behind a pillar. Lightsabers smashed together, sputtered and burned, then whisked apart. The air felt thicker, clogged with the energy of the battle.

For long minutes, the two students fought as if in a graceful dance. Obi-Wan leaped away from every attack and blocked every jarring blow. He did not try to hit Bruck.

Let him see that I'm not clumsy, Obi-Wan

thought bitterly. *Let him see that I'm not stupid. Let him see it over and over again.*

Sweat began to drench Obi-Wan's clothes. His muscles burned. He could hardly breathe fast enough to get the air he needed. But as long as he did not attack in anger, the Force remained strong with him. He tried not to think about the fight. He lost himself in the dance, and soon he felt so weary, he did not think at all.

Bruck fought slower and slower. Soon, Obi-Wan did not even need to leap away from Bruck's weary attacks. He merely blocked them, until finally Bruck gave up.

"Good, Obi-Wan," Yoda called. "Learning you are."

Obi-Wan switched off his lightsaber and hung it on his belt. He used the blindfold to wipe the sweat from his face. Next to him, Bruck was doubled over, panting. He did not look at Obi-Wan.

"You see," Yoda said. "To defeat an enemy, you do not have to kill. Defeat the rage that burns in him, and he is your enemy no longer. Rage the true enemy is."

Obi-Wan understood what Yoda meant. But Bruck's glazed glare told Obi-Wan that he had not defeated his opponent's anger. Nor had he won the boy's respect.

The two boys turned to Yoda and bowed

solemnly. A vision of his friend Bant rose in Obi-Wan's head. One of the best things about beating Bruck would be telling her about it.

"Enough for one day," Yoda said. "Tomorrow, a Jedi Knight comes to the Temple seeking a Padawan. Ready for him you must be."

Obi-Wan tried to hide his surprise. Usually, when a Knight came to the Temple in search of a Padawan, rumors beat the arrival by days. That way, if a student wanted to earn the honor of becoming the Knight's Padawan, he or she could prepare mentally and physically.

"Who?" Obi-Wan asked, heart racing. "Who's coming?"

"Seen him before, you have," Yoda said. "Master Qui-Gon Jinn."

Obi-Wan's hopes rose. Qui-Gon Jinn was a powerful Knight, one of the best. He had been to the Temple before to look at apprentices. Each time, he'd left without taking a new Padawan.

Obi-Wan had heard rumors that Qui-Gon had lost his last Padawan in a tremendous battle, and had vowed never to take another. He came to the Temple every year only because the Council of Masters asked him to. He would spend a few hours watching the pupils, studying them as if looking for something that no one else could see. Then he would leave, empty-handed, to fight the darkness alone.

Obi-Wan felt his hopes dim. Qui-Gon had rejected so many students. What made him think that he would be able to please him?

"He won't want me," Obi-Wan said in defeat. "He's seen me fight before, and he did not choose me then. No one will."

Yoda squinted up at Obi-Wan with wise eyes. "Hummmph! Always in motion the future is. One cannot be sure, but I have sensed . . . a kinder destiny for you."

Something in Yoda's tone made Obi-Wan wonder. "Will he choose me?" he asked.

"On Qui-Gon that depends — and you," Yoda said. "Come back tomorrow and fight for him with the Force as your ally. Perhaps accept you he will." Yoda put a comforting hand on his arm. "Either way, it matters not. Leave the Temple soon you shall. But tell you I must, to lose such an apt pupil, I am sorry."

Startled and pleased, Obi-Wan looked at Yoda. The Master's eyes glowed as he blinked at Obi-Wan. A compliment from Yoda was as rare as an expression of regret. That was what made his opinion so highly prized. At that moment, Obi-Wan felt that even if he didn't become a Knight, he had earned Yoda's respect. That was a great gift.

Yoda turned and walked from the training room, the echo of his small feet thumping on the floor. He rounded the doorway into the hall and was gone. The lights powered down automatically and the room grew dusky with shadows.

Behind Obi-Wan, Bruck began to laugh. "Don't get your hopes up, Oafy. Yoda is just trying to make you feel better. The Masters won't be able to push you onto anyone. There are plenty of better candidates than you."

Obi-Wan stiffened in anger. He felt tempted to point out that Bruck was *not* one of those better candidates. Instead, he headed for the doorway.

He had taken but a single step when something hard hit the back of his head. The sound of the blow against Obi-Wan's skull echoed through the room. Bruck had thrown a training probe.

As Obi-Wan spun to face Bruck, the boy powered up his lightsaber. Its red light cut through the gloom.

"Ready for another round?" Bruck asked.

Obi-Wan looked at the empty corridor. Yoda was gone. No one would see if he gave Bruck the beating he deserved. Bruck was often cruel, but usually not so brazen. He was deliberately provoking Obi-Wan, trying to get him to lose his temper.

But why? Obi-Wan wondered.

Of course! "You knew all along that Qui-Gon Jinn was coming to search for a Padawan, didn't you," Obi-Wan said slowly, as the suspicion hardened into certainty. Since Obi-Wan was the oldest apprentice in the Temple, the Jedi Masters would encourage Qui-Gon to take him — the lost cause. Bruck would not want that to happen.

Bruck laughed. "I made sure you didn't find out. If I'd had my way, you wouldn't have found out until he'd left."

Bruck hoped to become Qui-Gon's Padawan! And the only way to do it was to make sure that Obi-Wan failed. He'd tried to keep him from preparing, and now he was trying to make him mad. Obi-Wan's anger, his impatience, had been his downfall often enough in the past. Bruck hoped to fill his mind with rage and despair so that he would not be open to the Force.

Obi-Wan had been raised in the Jedi Temple since he was a baby. He hadn't seen much of greed or hatred or true evil. The Masters shielded the children from such things, to keep them from turning to the dark side of the Force.

Yet now Obi-Wan saw into the heart of ruthlessness. Bruck was plotting to steal his dreams.

He could not let him know how important Qui-Gon's visit was to him. He could not let Bruck know how he'd caused the fear to rise in him, fear that he would never be a Padawan.

Obi-Wan smiled. "Bruck, three months from

now, when you turn thirteen, I hope you'll make a great farmer." It was the worst insult that he could muster, to suggest that Bruck's mastery of the Force was so small that he would be fit only for the Agricultural Corps.

Bruck leaped toward him with a snarl, his lightsaber held high. Obi-Wan spun to meet him with a cry on his lips. Flashing blades clashed in a burst of light and buzzing sound as the boys met in the room's center.

Weary as they were, the boys fought until they could hardly move. By the time they crept from the training room, both boys were badly burned and bruised.

Neither had won, and both had lost.

As Obi-Wan headed to his chamber, Bruck took a lift to the upper rooms of the Temple, where the healers practiced their arts. He limped into the medic's chambers, pretending to be more hurt than he was. His clothes were slashed and singed from the practice sabers, and blood ran from his nose.

When the medics saw him, their first question was, "What happened?"

Bruck gasped, "Obi-Wan Kenobi . . ." and then pretended to faint.

One of the healers looked at him, then said brusquely to a droid, "Go notify the Masters."

CHAPTER 2

Obi-Wan Kenobi was bandaging his burns in his room when he got the bad news. He was trying to imagine ways to impress Qui-Gon in the morning. He considered ways to improve his fighting skills — anything he might say or do to convince the Knight that he was worthy to become a Jedi's Padawan Learner. But then Docent Vant brought a data pad and showed him his orders.

Suddenly all of his plans and dreams were shattered.

"Here now, it isn't that horrible," Docent Vant said. She was a tall blue-skinned woman with an elegant headtail that twitched nervously.

Obi-Wan stared at the orders in shock. The data pad told him that he would ship out of the Temple in the morning. He needed to pack his bags.

He was to report to the world of Bandomeer —

some planet he'd never even heard of, out on the Galactic Rim. There he would join the Agricultural Corps.

"But I don't understand," he said numbly. "I still have four weeks until my birthday."

"I know," Docent Vant said. "But your ship, the *Monument*, leaves tomorrow, with a thousand miners aboard. It can't wait just because you have a birthday."

In shock, Obi-Wan looked around at his room. Overhead, three model Verpine fighters droned near the ceiling. He'd made them himself. Repulsorlift fields held them aloft, and their running lights flashed purple and green as they hummed about. Miniature insectoid pilots swiveled their heads, as if to look around. Books and charts were piled on his study table. His lightsaber hung in its usual place on the wall. He couldn't imagine leaving here. It was his home. But he would leave it all gladly for the hard life of an apprentice. Not a farmer!

He would never be a Knight now. Bruck had been right, Obi-Wan thought bitterly. Yoda had been trying to make him feel better.

The shock and despair made him feel sick. He raised his gaze to Docent Vant. "I could still be a Jedi Knight."

Docent Vant touched Obi-Wan's hand tenderly. She smiled, revealing her pointed teeth.

She shook her head. "Not everyone is meant to be a warrior. The Republic needs healers and farmers, too. With your Force skills, you will be able to treat sick crops. Your talent will help feed whole worlds."

"But —" Obi-Wan wanted to say that he felt cheated. He deserved four more weeks. "It's a job for rejects, initiates too weak to be Knights. Besides, tomorrow Qui-Gon Jinn will be looking for a Padawan. Master Yoda said that I should fight for him."

Docent Vant shook her head. "That was before the Masters heard of the beating you gave to initiate Bruck. Did you really think that the healers would not tell what you had done?"

In dawning horror, Obi-Wan realized what had happened. Bruck had set the trap, and he had walked straight into it. He wanted to protest, to say that he was innocent. It had been a fair fight. And healers? Surely Bruck had not needed healers — except to back up whatever story he had told.

"This is not the first time that you have let your anger get the best of you," Docent Vant said. "But let us hope that it is the last." She nodded briskly. "Now, try not to look so sad. You will need to pack your bags and say good-bye to your friends tonight. The galaxy is a big place. They will want to see you before you go."

She left, closing the door softly behind her. Obi-Wan was left alone with only the sound of the model fighters flying overhead.

There was nothing else to do but pack his bags. Obi-Wan felt too devastated and ashamed to say good-bye. Not to Garen Muln or Reeft, or even to his best friend, Bant. They would feel angry and hurt if he left quietly, but he couldn't face them. His friends would want to know where he was going. Once he told them that he had been ordered to report to the Agricultural Corps, word would get around. He could imagine how some of the others would laugh. There was nothing he could say or do to clear his name.

Because the truth was that if Bruck had set the trap, he had walked into it willingly. Blindly and without thought, perhaps. But it was his own will that led him there. What kind of Jedi would he make if he could fall for the tricks of a bully like Bruck?

Obi-Wan threw himself back on his sleep-couch. He had let Master Yoda down. He had thrown away his one last chance by letting anger cloud his mind. Now his worst fear had come true. After all his years of training, he was not good enough to be a Jedi Knight.

Yoda had always told him that anger and fear

drove him too hard, that if he didn't learn to control them, they would lead him down a path he didn't want to follow. "Befriend them, you should," Yoda had advised. "Look them in the eye without blinking. Use faults as your teachers, you should. Then, rule you, they will not. Rule them, you shall."

Yoda's wisdom was engraved on his heart. How could he have failed to follow it?

Outside his door, he heard the rest of the initiates prepare for sleep. Goodnights were exchanged, shouted from chamber to chamber. Finally, the lights powered down, and the halls were silent.

Obi-Wan felt surrounded by the peaceful energy of the sleeping students. It did not soothe his raging heart. His fellow initiates could rest. They did not have thoughts that tormented them. Obi-Wan tossed and turned, unable to stop imagining the sight of Bruck's triumphant face when he learned of Obi-Wan's fate.

There was a soft knock at his door. Hesitantly, Obi-Wan rose and opened it. Bant stood, not saying a word, just looking at him. The young Calamarian girl wore a green robe that set off her salmon-colored skin. Her clothes smelled moist and salty, for she'd just come from her room, which was always kept as steamy as the air off a warm sea. She was small for her ten years of age, and she watched him steadily with her huge silver eyes.

She took in his bruises and burns, all with an expression that said, *You've been fighting again.* Then she looked past him, to his bags packed on the floor.

"You weren't going to say good-bye?" she asked, blinking back huge tears. "You were just going to leave?"

"I've been assigned to the Agricultural Corps," he said, hoping that she'd understand how humiliating it was for him. "I wanted to say good-bye, but . . ."

She shook her head. "I heard you are going to a planet called Bandomeer."

So everyone knew already. Obi-Wan nodded dully just as Bant lurched forward to give him a clumsy hug.

"Yes, that's where I'm going," he said. He hugged her. *So, my fate is decided,* he realized in despair. *I will be a farmer.* Because this first good-bye would be followed by others. He couldn't avoid them.

Bant frowned and stepped back. "It will be dangerous. Did they tell you it would be dangerous?"

Obi-Wan shook his head. "It's just the Agricultural Corps. How dangerous could it get?"

"We are not to know," Bant said.

"We are to do," Obi-Wan added softly. It was a phrase they had heard many times from the Masters, when they were asked to do tasks that they could not understand the significance of.

"Miss you, I will," Bant said, echoing Yoda's strange way of talking. She blinked back tears.

"So sorry, I am," Obi-Wan answered. He tried to smile, but could not. In answer, Bant hugged him again swiftly, then hurried away to hide her tears.

CHAPTER 3

With the help of Jedi healing techniques and the Temple's marvelous ointments, Obi-Wan Kenobi's burns and bruises were healed by morning. But the pain in his heart had not eased. He slept briefly, then rose well before dawn.

He said good-bye to Garen Muln and Reeft, two boys from different sides of the galaxy who had become inseparable in their years in the Jedi Temple.

All through the morning meal, Reeft, a Dresselian with an abnormally wrinkled face, kept saying to everyone at the table, "I don't mean to sound greedy, but may I have your meat?" or "I don't mean to sound greedy, but . . ." as he looked pointedly at some puff cake or drink. Though Obi-Wan had not had dinner the night before, he shared everything. Bant kindly handed over half her puff cake. With his leathery gray skin and all those wrinkles, the Dresselian could look awfully sad if he did not get everything he wanted to eat.

"It won't be so bad," Garen Muln told Obi-Wan. "At least you're going on an adventure." Garen Muln had always been restless. Yoda had often given him extra stillness exercises.

"And you'll be around food," Reeft added hopefully.

"Who knows where each of us will end up?" Bant added. "The missions to come will be different for each of us."

"And unexpected," Garen Muln agreed. "That's what Yoda says. Not everyone is meant to be an apprentice."

Obi-Wan nodded. It was good that he'd given Reeft most of his food. He couldn't eat. He knew his friends were trying to make him feel better. But they still had plenty of chances to become Jedi. That highest honor was what they all wanted, all they worked for. No matter what they said, they all knew his lost chance was a crushing disappointment.

Around him, Obi-Wan heard the swirl of conversations at the other tables. Students looked over at him, then looked away. Most gazes were compassionate, and some tried to cheer him. But he sensed the overwhelming feeling in the room was that everyone was glad that what had happened to Obi-Wan had not happened to them.

At Bruck's table, the voices were loud and reached their ears. "Always knew he wouldn't make it," Bruck's friend Aalto said loudly. Obi-Wan's ears burned as he heard Bruck's high snicker. He turned, and Bruck stared at him, daring him to pick another fight.

"Don't mind him," Bant said. "He's a fool."

Obi-Wan turned away and finished his meal, just as a huge black Barabel fruit plopped on the table near his tray. Juice from the fruit splattered on Bant and Garen Muln. Obi-Wan glared over at Bruck, who had come halfway across the room to throw it.

"Plant it, Oafy," Bruck said. "I hear they'll grow just about anywhere."

Obi-Wan started to rise from his chair, but Bant put her hand over his and held him down, trying to calm him.

Obi-Wan smiled at Bruck, keeping himself in control. *He wants to anger me,* Obi-Wan knew. *He hopes to anger me. How often in the past have others played me like this, making me lose the chance to become a Padawan?*

Obi-Wan held in his anger, and merely smiled at Bruck. Yet a white-hot fury was building inside him.

Just then, Reeft muttered, "I don't mean to sound greedy, but are you going to eat that Barabel fruit?"

Obi-Wan nearly burst out laughing. "Thank you, Bruck," he said, scraping the fruit off the table and placing it in a cup. "The people of Bandomeer will be honored when I share with them your gift — the gift of one farmer to another."

In an upper room of the Jedi Temple, Master Yoda argued with the senior members of the Jedi Council. They were meditating in a huge greenhouse, the Room of a Thousand Fountains, where fountains and waterfalls streamed through an emerald forest.

Outside, the surface of Coruscant was hidden by black storm clouds.

"Obi-Wan Kenobi must be allowed to fight before Qui-Gon Jinn this day," Master Yoda said, just as a bolt of lightning snarled through the clouds below. "I have foreseen it."

"What?" Senior Councilor Mace Windu asked. He was a strong, dark-skinned man with a shaved head. He studied Yoda with eyes that could pierce like blaster bolts. "What would be the point? Obi-Wan has proven once again that he cannot control his anger or his impatience. And Qui-Gon Jinn is not ready for another impatient Padawan."

"Agreed," Yoda said. "Neither Obi-Wan nor Qui-Gon ready are. But the Force may yet bring Master and student together."

Mace Windu asked, "And what of last night, the beating that Obi-Wan gave to Bruck?"

Yoda waved his hand and, as he did so, a referee droid appeared from behind the bushes.

"Advanced Jedi Training Droid 6, last night the fight you saw," Yoda prompted.

"Obi-Wan's heart was beating at sixty-eight beats per minute," the droid reported. "His torso was faced northeast at twenty-seven degrees, with right hand extended down, clutching his training saber. His body temperature was —"

Mace Windu sighed. If allowed to continue, the training droid would take an hour just to describe how Obi-Wan had crossed the room.

"Just tell us who provoked the fight," Mace Windu said. "Who said what, and then what happened?"

The training droid AJTD6 gave an indignant buzz at being curtailed. But after a glower from Mace Windu, it began the story of how Bruck had provoked Obi-Wan into the fight.

At the conclusion, Mace Windu sighed. "So we have one deceitful boy, and one foolish one," he said. He looked at Master Yoda. "What do you suggest?"

Yoda blinked. "Give both a chance to fail again, we should," he said.

CHAPTER 4

Bruck's red lightsaber crackled and hissed as Obi-Wan desperately tried to parry with his own. For the fourth time in less than a day the two boys were locked in combat, grunting and struggling.

Obi-Wan's muscles ached. Sweat drenched his thick tunic. Bruck's toughness surprised him. The boy was fighting desperately, as though his life depended on it. Obi-Wan realized that Bruck was just as afraid of not being chosen as a Jedi apprentice as he was.

But Obi-Wan would match Bruck's toughness with his own, and then push even harder. This was his one last chance.

Bruck's blade hummed as it angled toward Obi-Wan's throat. A touch there would signal a killing blow, and Obi-Wan would lose the bout.

A cry rose up from the crowd seated in the

shadows surrounding the battle arena. Masters and students had gathered to watch the fight. Obi-Wan could not see them — he could only hear their shouts and encouragement. Overhead, AJTD6 whisked around, monitoring the match as referee.

"Fool." Bruck growled softly enough so that others could not hear above the cheering. "You should never have agreed to fight me. You can't win."

Bruck's shocking white hair was tied in a ponytail, and sweat stood out in droplets on his brow. He wore heavily padded black body armor. The odor of burned flesh and singed hair hung heavily in the air. Both warriors had managed to hit one another, but the touches so far had not been firm strikes.

Around the arena, many of the younger initiates cheered, calling out encouragement to Bruck or Obi-Wan. All of them had heard of the fight last night. Obi-Wan heard Bant shout "Courage, Obi-Wan! You're doing well!" Garen Muln whistled through his teeth.

"You mean that *you* can't win!" Obi-Wan told Bruck scornfully as their training lightsabers tangled and sizzled. "Your failure today will signal to everyone that you are not just a loser, but a liar."

The Masters had decided the fight would be without blindfolds. Bruck's face was close, and his eyes glared at Obi-Wan with hate. The moment stretched, extended. In Bruck's eyes Obi-Wan saw a future mapped out for him, a future in which anger ruled him and he began to hate all who opposed him.

Obi-Wan reached out for the Force. He felt it flow around him, but he could not fully grasp it. Here was the boy who stood between him and his dream, who mocked him, who tricked him. He pushed against Bruck and saw the surprise in the boy's eyes as he fell backward.

Obi-Wan took advantage of Bruck's uncertainty to aim a sizzling attack at Bruck's face. Bruck ducked and slashed at Obi-Wan's feet. Obi-Wan leaped high in the air.

As a child, Obi-Wan had learned by fighting older students to avoid flashy attacks that wasted energy. Instead, he'd been trained to fight defensively, to block blows with small movements, or to avoid them.

As Obi-Wan parried Bruck's moves, he felt Qui-Gon Jinn's eyes on him. The Jedi was a rebel and a loner, and Obi-Wan wanted to be seen as a rebel, too.

Instead of waiting to gauge Bruck's attack strategy, Obi-Wan attacked suddenly and furiously. Bruck tried to block the attacks, but Obi-Wan's lightsaber met Bruck's with stinging power. Bruck nearly dropped his weapon.

Obi-Wan brandished his lightsaber in both hands, swinging brutally. Bruck tried to block a second time, and fell back, sprawling. His lightsaber switched off and went skittering over the uneven floor.

Obi-Wan slammed down, a decisive blow that should have won the bout, but Bruck managed to roll aside and grab his lightsaber. He barely had time to switch it on before Obi-Wan's lightsaber battered down again.

This time, there was no blocking the blow. Bruck's lightsaber was knocked back into him. Obi Wan caught Bruck cleanly between the eyes, burning his hair and scorching his skin.

Bruck cried out in pain as both lightsabers burned him, and Yoda announced, "Enough!"

All around the arena, the initiates shouted and cheered. Bant's eyes were shining, and Reeft's wrinkled face held more creases due to his wide smile.

Obi-Wan backed away, panting. Sweat ran down his arms and face; his muscles ached from exertion. His head swam with dizziness.

Yet he had never tasted such sweet triumph. He glanced into the shadows around the arena, and saw Qui-Gon Jinn watching him. The Jedi

Master gave him the briefest nod, then began speaking to Yoda.

I've won, Obi-Wan realized, a thrill rising within him. *I beat Bruck soundly. Qui-Gon is impressed.*

He tried to keep his rising exhilaration in check. He bowed to Yoda and the rest of the Masters. Then he couldn't resist raising his lightsaber in the air to the cheers of his friends. Obi-Wan grinned and shook the lightsaber at a proud Bant, Reeft, and Garen Muln. Perhaps he'd won more than an important fight. Perhaps he had won the right to become a Padawan.

The cheers still rang in his ears as he went to the dressing chamber. He showered and changed into a fresh tunic. He was tossing his stained tunic into the laundry container when Qui-Gon Jinn entered the room. He was a big, powerful man, but his footsteps were soundless.

"Who taught you to fight like that?" Qui-Gon asked. The Jedi had rough features, but his was a sensitive, thoughtful face.

"What do you mean?"

"Students in the Temple rarely attack so viciously. They learn to defend, to wear one another down. They conserve their strength. Yet you fought . . . like a very dangerous man. You left yourself open to attack time and again, and relied upon the other boy to take the defensive stance."

"I wanted to end it quickly," Obi-Wan said. "The Force allowed it."

Qui-Gon studied Obi-Wan for a long moment. "I am not so sure. You cannot always rely upon your enemy to take the defensive stance. Your fighting style is dangerous, too risky."

"You could teach me better," Obi-Wan said evenly. The words invited the Jedi to ask Obi-Wan to be his Padawan.

But Qui-Gon merely bowed his head in thought. "Perhaps I could," he said slowly. The words caused a hope to rise in Obi-Wan. But only a heartbeat later, it was dashed.

"Or perhaps no one could," Qui-Gon continued. "You were angry with the other boy. I sensed anger in both of you."

"That's not why I wanted to win." Obi-Wan held Qui-Gon's gaze steadily, letting him know that he had fought to impress him, to show him how well he could serve him.

Qui-Gon watched Obi-Wan intently for a long moment, still staring at him . . . *through* him. Hope rose in Obi-Wan again. *He'll ask me now*, Obi-Wan thought. *He'll ask me to be his Padawan*.

But Qui-Gon merely said, "In future fights, rein in your anger. A Jedi Knight never exhausts himself when battling a stronger foe. And never expect your enemy to miss an opportunity to do you harm."

Qui-Gon turned and headed for the door.

Obi-Wan stood still, confused. Qui-Gon was not taking him as his apprentice. He was merely giving out advice, the way the Masters always did.

Obi-Wan couldn't let him walk away. He couldn't see his dream die.

"Wait!" Obi-Wan called out. When Qui-Gon turned, he dropped to one knee as a sign of humility. "If I was wrong, it only means I need the best teacher. Will you take me with you?"

Qui-Gon turned slowly, and eyed the boy. He frowned, deep in thought. At last he murmured, "No."

"Qui-Gon Jinn, I will be thirteen in four weeks," Obi-Wan said. The truth was a desperate gamble, but he had to say it. "You are my last chance to be a Jedi Knight."

Qui-Gon shook his head sadly. "It is better not to train a boy to become a Knight if he has so much anger. There is the risk he will turn to the dark side."

With that, the huge Jedi wheeled and strode for the door, his cape streaming.

Obi-Wan sprang to his feet. "I won't turn," he said with certainty.

But Qui-Gon neither slowed his stride nor turned back. In a moment he was gone, as quickly and silently as he had appeared.

For a long minute, Obi-Wan could only stare at the empty air in shock. At first, he couldn't quite take it in. It was over. His last chance had played out. There was nothing left for him.

His bags were packed, sitting on a bench. He had only to pick them up and take them to the transport that would carry him to the planet Bandomeer.

He lifted his chin. Though he would never become a Knight, he would at least leave the Temple like one. He would not plead. He picked up his bags and headed down the long hallway that led from the battle arena to the landing platform.

He passed the meditation grotto, the meal room, the classrooms. Places where he had learned, struggled, and triumphed.

It was all home to him. Now he must leave and head for a future he hadn't asked for and did not want.

Obi-Wan walked out the door of the Temple for the last time. He tried to push away his deep sorrow and look to the future as he'd been taught.

But he could not.

CHAPTER 5

Qui-Gon Jinn could not get the sight of Obi-Wan's despairing face out of his mind. The boy had struggled not to show it, but it was written on his every feature.

Qui-Gon sat quietly in the star map room. Among all the rooms at the Temple, this was his favorite. A velvety blue ceiling curved above him in a dome. The only light came from the stars and planets that surrounded him, pin-pricks against the blue in all the glowing colors of the spectrum. He had only to reach out a hand and touch a planet for a hologram to appear, detailing its physical properties, its surrounding satellites, and its form of government.

Knowledge was so easily obtained here. But when it came to the heart, so much was a mystery.

Qui-Gon told himself that he had made the correct decision. The only decision. The boy fought well, but too fiercely. There was danger there.

"The boy is not my responsibility," Qui-Gon said aloud.

"Certain are you?" Yoda asked from behind him.

Qui-Gon turned, startled. "I didn't hear you," he said politely.

Yoda walked farther into the star map room. "A dozen boys fought for you. If you do not choose a Padawan today, the dreams of at least one of those boys will die."

Sighing, Qui-Gon studied a bright red star. "There will be more boys next year. Perhaps then I will choose a Padawan." In his visits to the Temple, Qui-Gon always valued his time spent with Yoda. Now he wished the Master would go away. He did not want to discuss this. But he knew Yoda would not leave until he had made his point.

"Perhaps," Yoda agreed. "Or perhaps still reluctant, you will be. What of young Obi-Wan? Well he fought."

"He fought . . . ferociously," Qui-Gon agreed.

"Yes," Yoda said. "Like a boy that I knew long ago —"

"Don't," Qui-Gon interrupted. "Xanatos is gone. I don't want to be reminded."

"Not speaking of that one," Yoda said. "Of *you* I spoke."

Qui-Gon didn't answer. Yoda knew him too well. He could not argue.

"Strong in the Force he is," Yoda remarked.

"And angry and reckless," Qui-Gon said, a trace of irritation beginning to edge his tone. "And likely to turn."

"Not all angry young men to the dark side turn," Yoda said calmly. "Not if a proper teacher they have."

"I will not take him, Master Yoda," Qui-Gon said evenly. He knew Yoda would hear the strong will in his words.

"Very well," Yoda said. "But by chance alone we do not live our lives. If take an apprentice you will not, then, in time, perhaps fate will choose."

"Perhaps," Qui-Gon agreed. He hesitated. "What will happen to the boy?"

"For the Agricultural Corps he will work."

Qui-Gon grunted. "A farmer?" *Such a waste of potential.* "Tell him . . . that I wish him luck."

"Too late," Yoda said. "On his way to Bandomeer he is."

"Bandomeer?" Qui-Gon asked in surprise.

"Know the place you do?"

"Know it? The Senate has asked me to go

there. I'm leaving now. You knew this, didn't you?" Qui-Gon eyed the small Master suspiciously.

"Hmmm . . ." Yoda said. "I knew it not. But more than coincidence this is. Strange are the ways of the Force."

"But why send the boy to Bandomeer?" Qui-Gon asked. "It's a brutal world. If the weather doesn't kill him, the predators will. He'll need all of his skill just to stay alive — never mind the Agri-Corps!"

"Yes, so the Council thought," Yoda said. "Good to grow crops Bandomeer may not be. But a good place for a young Jedi to grow it *is*."

"If he doesn't get himself killed," Qui-Gon growled. "You must have more faith in him than I do."

"Yes my point that is," Master Yoda said, chuckling. "Listen harder, you must."

With an exasperated sigh, Qui-Gon returned his attention to the stars.

"Study the stars you may, Qui-Gon," Yoda said as he left. "They have much to teach you. But will it be what you need to learn?"

CHAPTER 6

The *Monument* was an old Corellian barge, pocked and scarred from meteor hits. It was shaped like a crate, and attached to the front of it were a dozen cargo boxes it would push to Bandomeer. It was the ugliest, dirtiest ship that Obi-Wan could have imagined.

If the exterior was ugly, the interior was foul. Its battered corridors smelled of miners' dust and the sweaty bodies of many species. Repair ports were left open, so that wires and pressure hoses — the ship's guts — spilled out as if from an open wound.

Everywhere on the *Monument* enormous Hutts slithered about like giant slugs. Whiphids stalked the corridors with their moldy fur and tusks. Tall Arconans with triangular heads and glittering eyes moved in small groups.

Obi-Wan wandered in a daze, his bags in hand. No one had been at the entry port to guide him. No one even seemed to notice him. He realized gloomily that he had left behind the data pad Docent Vant had given him. On it was his room number.

He looked for a crew member, but he could only find miners being transported to Bandomeer. Obi-Wan trudged on with gathering despair. The ship was strange and frightening. It was so different from the hushed, gleaming hallways of the Temple, where he could hear the sound of fountains wherever he walked. He knew every corner of the Temple, knew the fastest route to get from the arena, where they practiced tumbling and balance, to the pool, where he would dive from the highest tower. . . .

Obi-Wan's steps grew slower and slower. What was Bant doing now? Was she in class, or a private tutorial? Was she swimming in the pool with Reeft and Garen Muln? If his friends were thinking of him, they would never imagine what a horrible place he had landed in.

Suddenly, a huge Hutt blocked his path. Before Obi-Wan could say a word, the Hutt grabbed him by the throat and threw him against a wall.

"Where do you think you're going, slug?"

"Uh, what?" Obi-Wan asked in surprise. What had he done wrong? He was just trudging down the hall. With a sense of unease, he noticed that two particularly evil-looking Whiphids stood behind the Hutt. "B-Bandomeer," he stammered.

The Hutt studied Obi-Wan as if he were a morsel of food. The creature's huge tongue rolled from its mouth and slid over its gray lips, leaving a trail of slime.

"That's not a ship's uniform you're wearing, and you're not Offworld."

Obi-Wan looked down at his clothes. He wore a loose gray tunic. He suddenly realized that the Hutt in front of him wore a black triangular patch that showed a bright red planet, like an eye. A silver spaceship circling the planet became the iris of the eye. Beneath the logo were the words *Offworld Mining*. The Whiphids wore the same symbol.

"He must be from that other outfit," a Whiphid said.

"Maybe he's a spy," the second Whiphid growled. "What's he got in those bags, you think? Bombs?"

The Hutt pushed his huge, grotesque face close to Obi-Wan's. "Any miner who doesn't work for Offworld is the enemy," he roared, shaking Obi-Wan roughly. "You, slug, are an enemy. And we don't allow the enemy on Offworld turf."

The Hutt's fingers were like huge slabs of meat. They tightened around Obi-Wan's neck, strangling him. Choking, Obi-Wan dropped his bags and grasped the Hutt's fingers. His lungs burned and the room spun.

Using all his strength, Obi-Wan managed to pry the Hutt's fingers from his throat long enough to gasp a breath. He stared into the cruel, blank eyes of the Hutt, trying to summon his Force powers.

"Leave me alone," Obi-Wan gasped, struggling to breathe. He let the Force carry the command to the Hutt, to batter his will, change his mind. This was not like fighting another student. He sensed a cruelty without conscience. There were no rules here, no Yoda to call off the fight.

"Leave you alone? Why?" the Hutt roared with cruel amusement.

I'm getting off to a good start, Obi-Wan thought despairingly.

The last thing he remembered was the Hutt's fist coming straight at him.

CHAPTER 7

Obi-Wan woke on a cot in a warm, well-lit room. His vision was blurry, and his head swam. A medical droid leaned over him, applying flesh glue to his cuts, checking for broken bones.

A young Human woman with reddish-brown hair and green eyes stood across the room, watching him. "Didn't anyone ever tell you not to tangle with a Hutt?" she asked.

Obi-Wan tried to shake his head, but even a tiny movement rocked him with pain. He took a long breath. He called on his Jedi training to accept the pain as a signal his body was sending. He had to accept the pain, respect it, not fight it. Then he'd have to ask his body to begin to heal.

Once he centered his mind, the pain seemed to ease. He turned to the woman. "I didn't seem to have a choice."

"I know what you mean." The woman flashed

him a brief grin. "Well, you survived. That's something." She walked closer to his bedside. "You're lucky I found you when I did. You're not one of ours."

"Ours?" Obi-Wan asked. He squinted at her. She wore an orange worksuit with a green triangle on it.

"We're the Arcona Mineral Harvest Corporation," the woman responded. "If you don't work for us, why did the Offworlders beat you?"

Obi-Wan tried to shrug, but pain shot through his shoulder. Sometimes it was hard to respect his body's signal. "You tell me. I was only looking for my cabin."

"You're a tough one," the woman said cheerfully. "Not everybody could withstand a pounding by a Hutt. Did you come on board looking for a job? We could use you at Arcona Harvest. I'm Clat'Ha, chief operations manager." She looked young to be running a mining operation — perhaps twenty-five.

"Have a job," Obi-Wan said, trying to feel his mouth with his tongue. He was relieved to feel that all his teeth were still in. "I'm Obi-Wan Kenobi. I'm with the Agricultural Corps."

Clat'Ha's mouth fell open. "You're the young Jedi? The ship's crew has been looking everywhere for you."

He tried to sit up, but Clat'Ha briskly pushed

him back. "Stay down. You're not ready to get up yet."

He laid back and Clat'Ha withdrew. "Good luck to you, Obi-Wan Kenobi," she said. "Watch yourself. You've stepped into the middle of a war. You're lucky to be alive. You may not be so lucky next time." She turned to leave, but Obi-Wan touched her hand.

"Wait," he said. "I don't understand. What war? Who's fighting?"

"Offworld's war," Clat'Ha answered. "You must have heard of them."

Obi-Wan shook his head. How could he explain that he'd lived his whole life in the Jedi Temple? He knew more about the ways of the Force than the ways of the universe.

"Offworld is one of the oldest and richest mining companies in the galaxy," Clat'Ha told him. "And they didn't get that way by letting others compete with them. Miners who get in their way tend to die."

"Who's their leader?" Obi-Wan asked.

"No one knows who owns Offworld," Clat'Ha said. "Someone who has been around for centuries, probably. And I'm not even sure that we could prove he or she is responsible for the murders. But the leader on the ship going to Bandomeer is a particularly ruthless Hutt by the name of Jemba."

Obi-Wan repeated the name in his mind. *Jemba*. It might have been Jemba who had beaten him. "Ruthless? In what way?"

Clat'Ha glanced over her shoulder, worried that someone would hear. "Offworld uses the cheapest labor possible. Out on the Rim worlds, in places like Bandomeer, half of Jemba's workers will be Whiphid slaves. But that's not the worst," Clat'Ha said. She hesitated.

"What's the worst?" Obi-Wan asked.

Clat'Ha's dark eyes flashed. "About five years ago, Jemba was Offworld's chieftain on the planet Varristad, where another startup mining firm was also working. Varristad is a small planet, without any air, so the workers all lived in a huge underground dome. Someone or something popped a hole in that dome, instantly destroying the artificial atmosphere. A quarter of a million people were killed. No one was ever able to prove that Jemba did it, but when the other company went bankrupt, he bought the mineral rights for practically nothing. He made a huge profit for Offworld. Now we'll have to deal with him on Bandomeer."

Obi-Wan said, "Are you certain it was intentional? Maybe it was an accident."

Clat'Ha looked unconvinced. "Maybe," she said. "But accidents follow Jemba the way that stink follows Whiphids — accidents like the one that happened to you. So take care."

There was something she hadn't told him. Obi-Wan could sense it — old pain and fear, the desire for revenge. "Who did you know on Varristad?" he asked.

Clat'Ha opened her mouth in surprise. Stubbornly, she shook her head. "No one," she lied.

He locked eyes with her. "Clat'Ha, we can't let this continue. The *Monument* isn't Offworld's ship! They can't just go around beating people up."

Clat'Ha sighed. "Maybe it isn't their ship, but Offworld's miners outnumber the crew thirty to one. The captain won't be able to do much to protect you. So if I were you, I'd stay off their turf. You're welcome on our side of the ship anytime." She headed for the door, then turned and flashed the grin that made her serious face look suddenly young and mischievous. "If you can find it."

Obi-Wan grinned back. But he still struggled against Clat'Ha's acceptance of the injustice. He didn't understand it. He had grown up in a world where disputes were mediated and resolved. No obvious injustice was allowed to stand.

"Clat'Ha, this isn't right," he said gravely.

"Why should we have to stay off their side of the ship? Why should you accept that?"

Clat'Ha's face flushed. "Because I don't want them on *my* side of the ship! Obi-Wan, listen to me," she said urgently. "Accidents happen around Jemba. Drilling rigs blow and tunnels collapse and people die. I don't want his corporate spies and saboteurs on my side of the *Monument*, any more than he would want mine on his. So just accept the way things are. It's better for everyone."

She left the room, the door swinging shut behind her. The edges of the door seemed to vibrate strangely. Obi-Wan realized that the heat he felt wasn't only because he was angry at injustice. His body was on fire. He tried to accept the fire and the pain, but dizziness overcame him. He fell back on his cot, head reeling, while the room spun.

CHAPTER 8

Obi-Wan dreamed that he was in the Jedi Temple, walking among the star maps. He reached out and touched the star closest to Bandomeer, one of a pair of giant dull red lights. A hologram appeared, and a Master long dead announced, "Bandomeer: the place where you will die if you're not careful."

He woke in the sickbay, with tubes in his arms and an oxygen mask over his nose and mouth. For a moment he thought he was still dreaming — Qui-Gon Jinn stood over him. Then the Jedi's large, cool hand rested on Obi-Wan's forehead, and Obi-Wan realized he was awake.

"H-how?" Obi-Wan whispered.

Qui-Gon's hand dropped, and he took a step back. "Don't try to speak," he said gently. "You've had a bad fever, but I've taken care of it. Your wounds turned out to be worse than what the medics could handle."

"Is it really you?" Obi-Wan asked, struggling to clear his clouded brain.

Qui-Gon smiled. It was the first time Obi-Wan had seen him smile, and he realized that Qui-Gon was not all coolness and judgment. "Yes, it's really me," he said.

"Did you come to look for me?" Obi-Wan asked hopefully. He would not have asked such a blunt question, but he was too weak to puzzle out why the Jedi was here.

Qui-Gon shook his head. "I'm on my way to Bandomeer as well. I'm on a mission for the Galactic Senate. Our missions have nothing to do with each other."

"Still, we're together," Obi-Wan said. "You could show me —"

But Qui-Gon shook his head once again. "No, Obi-Wan, that is not why I'm here. Our destinies lie along different paths. Now is the time for you to get to know the people that you will serve. You must forget about me. You must serve the Jedi in ways other than as a Knight. There is honor in that, too."

He did not say it cruelly. But Qui-Gon's words struck Obi-Wan like a blow. It seemed that every time his hopes were raised, they were dashed again.

It was clear to Obi-Wan that even though

chance had placed them on the same ship, Qui-Gon wanted nothing to do with him. If the rumors were true, then Obi-Wan, or any initiate Obi-Wan's age, would only be a painful reminder of the Padawan that Qui-Gon had lost. Obi-Wan could not fight Qui-Gon's past.

He hid his disappointment and tried to look strong, despite his physical weakness. "I see," Obi-Wan said.

The door to the sickbay opened a crack. A triangular head appeared in the crack, and glowing green eyes peered at Obi-Wan. As soon as the intruder saw that Obi-Wan had noticed him, the door swished shut.

Obi-Wan turned back to Qui-Gon. "You're right. My mission should be my first concern. I'll —" He stopped when the door opened a crack again. Obi-Wan struggled to raise himself on his elbows. "Well, come in!" he called to the intruder.

An Arconan edged into the room. He was slightly shorter than most, with skin that was more green than gray. "We did not mean to disturb —"

"It's all right," Obi-Wan said kindly.

"— but we were told to meet Clat'Ha here. She has a situation she needs to discuss. We heard that a young boy faced a Hutt in a great battle, and survived," the Arconan said softly. "We wanted to see the great hero. We are sorry to disturb. We will wait outside." He began to retreat.

Obi-Wan looked over the Arconan's shoulder before he remembered that Arconans always referred to themselves as "we." They did not have a sense of an individual self and lived all their lives in colonies.

"I think I'd better set you straight," Obi-Wan said. "First of all, it wasn't a great battle. The Hutt just picked me up and strangled me until I passed out. I'm no hero."

"That you survived at all is a credit," Qui-Gon observed.

"Exactly." The Arconan took several steps forward. "The Hutts inspire great terror in us. You showed strength and courage. We admire that. You *are* a hero."

Obi-Wan looked at Qui-Gon helplessly. He realized that he couldn't talk the Arconan out of his overblown opinion. Qui-Gon turned away to hide a smile.

"Well, sit down and introduce yourself," Obi-Wan said. "In this place, I need all the friends I can get."

"Our name is Si Treemba," the Arconan said, perching on a chair. "We know yours is Obi-

Wan Kenobi. We would be honored to be your friend."

The door to the sickbay slid open. Clat'Ha strode in with an impatient expression.

"Good, you're here," she said to Si Treemba.

Si Treemba scrambled to his feet. "We —" he began, but Clat'Ha cut him off by turning to Qui-Gon.

"We have a problem," she said crisply. "Someone has been tampering with our equipment. Young Si Treemba here discovered it on a routine inspection. We have three Arconan tunneling machines in stock, and all three have been sabotaged."

"How so?" Qui-Gon asked.

Si Treemba stepped forward. "The thermocoms that monitor the tunnelers' hull temperature have been removed, sir. And the coring couplers have been rigged so that they will not disengage."

"What does that mean?" Obi-Wan asked.

Qui-Gon thought for a minute. "The Arconan tunnelers are vehicles that drill through rock and soil. As they do, the friction of the hull moving past all that stone makes the vehicle very hot. Without the thermocoms, the cooling system would not work. And with the coring couplers sabotaged, the driver of the tunneler would not be able to shut it off. The machine would simply keep digging until it melted from the heat. Everyone in it would die."

"Exactly," Clat'Ha said grimly. "I think that we know who is responsible."

A booming voice came from the doorway, speaking in Huttese. *"Sie batha ne beechee ta Jemba?" Are you talking about me, the Great Jemba?*

The Hutt outside the door was much larger than the one that had beaten Obi-Wan. Hutts can live for hundreds of years, and they never really stop growing — either in size or cunning. This one, Jemba, had a mouth so vast that he could have swallowed three men whole. Jemba's huge face and eyes filled the doorway.

"Yes," Qui-Gon said evenly, "we were talking about you, O Great Jemba. Come in — if you can."

Jemba hunkered down. "It has been many years since I could squeeze through such a small hole, Jedi," Jemba boomed. "Why don't you come out here?" He licked his lips.

Qui-Gon walked to the doorway and faced the Hutt. "You have been accused of sabotaging the Arconans' tunnelers."

"Aaaagh!" Jemba said, drawing back a pace. He placed a hand over his uppermost heart, a

Huttese gesture meant to indicate his innocence. "Never! I swear, Jedi, I did not do it. Do I look like the kind of creature who would sneak around, sabotaging other people's equipment?"

Obi-Wan did not believe the Hutt for a moment, but he almost had to laugh at the idea that the enormous Hutt could *sneak* anywhere.

"Of course I don't believe that you did it, personally, Great One," Qui-Gon said. "But one of your crew could have, under your direction."

"Aaaagh! Aaaagh!" Jemba squirmed backward like a giant worm and pounded his hand on his uppermost heart again. "I am hurt by such accusations! I know nothing of this matter. Look into my hearts, Jedi, and you will see that I do not lie! Why does everyone think I am evil, just because I am a Hutt?" Jemba demanded. "I am an honest businessman."

"Enough of this," Clat'Ha said in disgust. She strode forward to face Jemba, her hands on her hips, just above the blaster strapped to her left leg. "Of course it was one of your crew!"

"I swear, I know nothing of this matter!" Jemba roared.

Clat'Ha reached for her blaster.

Qui-Gon raised a hand, warning her back.

"Perhaps," Jemba said, his eyes narrowing

craftily, "your people did it to hurt *me*. Your unreasonable hatred for me is well-known. You have already asked the mining guild to have Offworld banned from Bandomeer. Now, by casting suspicion on me and my crew, you hope to have me lawfully removed."

"I don't care whether you are removed lawfully or not," Clat'Ha said furiously. "I just want you gone!"

"Exactly!" Jemba roared. The huge Hutt looked imploringly at Qui-Gon. "You see what I am faced with? How can a Hutt fight such unreasonable hatred?"

"Excuse me, Jemba," Clat'Ha said in a mock politeness. "But it's not *unreasonable* to hate a lying, scheming, cowardly murderer."

The Hutt's enormous body suddenly puffed in indignation. "We have not even reached Bandomeer," Jemba said, "and this woman tries to discredit me before the mining guild. Now she tries to frame me! Listen to how she talks to me. There is no respect in her voice!"

"I may not respect you, Jemba," Clat'Ha spat back, "but I certainly didn't frame you. Your lies are as pathetic as your denials."

Jemba gave a roar of anger and launched himself at Clat'Ha. He hit the door frame, which began to crack and splinter under the pressure. Si Treemba, terrified, hissed and pressed himself against the wall. Obi-Wan watched in fascination. The Hutt could bring down the entire sickbay!

Clat'Ha drew her blaster, but Qui-Gon stepped in front of her and raised his hand. He locked eyes with the Hutt. Obi-Wan felt the power of the Force fill the room.

"Enough," Qui-Gon said quietly.

Jemba stopped pushing to get inside the room. The Hutt knew he could not get to Clat'Ha. Qui-Gon glanced at Clat'Ha. Slowly, she lowered her blaster and returned it to the holding device on her leg. Obi-Wan had to admire Qui-Gon's skill. He felt a pang of regret. There was so much he wished he could learn from the Jedi.

"Now," Qui-Gon said in a reasonable tone, "let us review the situation. The machines were sabotaged. Yet both of you insist you did not do it. There is nowhere to take this except open warfare." Qui-Gon looked at each of them in turn. "And that is something that neither of you wish for, I'm sure."

"Jedi," Jemba said, "you think yourself to be a fair man. But when Hutts and Humans argue, even the fairest of men join sides against my kind." The Hutt's voice boomed in a tone of pure venom. "If it is war that she wants, then war will come. And if you take *her* side, I swear,

I will squash you like a pta fruit! Your Jedi status does not protect you!"

Menace hung thick in the air. It was clear that the Hutt meant everything he said. He was willing to kill anyone who stood against him. Obi-Wan had never encountered a creature of such malice.

It would be so easy to solve the situation, Obi-Wan thought. The Hutt was vulnerable, trapped in the small hallway outside the sickbay. Qui-Gon could draw his lightsaber, lunge forward, and slice the Hutt in half.

But Qui-Gon merely nodded his head graciously. "Thank you for the warning," he said simply.

Of course, Obi-Wan realized. *The warning is a gift.*

Jemba nodded as if satisfied, then slithered down the hall. Clat'Ha let out a long breath.

"Well, that went well," she muttered. She hurried to the door. "I have to warn my people. If this isn't war, it's something close to it." Clat'Ha raced out.

Qui-Gon shook his head sadly. "There is a strong hatred between those two. Neither of them will listen."

"I don't understand," Obi-Wan said. "Why did you let the Hutt go? He may be innocent of the crime of which he has been accused. But I'm sure he's guilty of others."

"Yes, he's guilty," Qui-Gon agreed. "But Clat'Ha can defend herself. As Jedi, we are bound to defend only those who have no other means of defense."

"Still, one of Jemba's crew has to have sabotaged those tunnelers. Why doesn't he try to find out who did it?" Obi-Wan asked.

Qui-Gon answered, "Because if one of Jemba's men did do it, it will make him look bad before the miners' guild. He might be ordered off Bandomeer permanently. He knows that, so he won't point any fingers at his own."

"Ah," Si Treemba said. "And Clat'Ha must feel the same. If anyone learned that one of her workers tried to frame Jemba, the miners' guild would be furious."

"But it shouldn't be hard to find out who really sabotaged the tunnelers," Obi-Wan pointed out excitedly.

Qui-Gon cocked his eyebrow. "This is not your affair," he warned. "If you went looking for those thermocoms, all you would find is trouble. You must stay out of it. And stay away from the Offworld side of the ship. You're not fully recovered yet, Obi-Wan."

With that, Qui-Gon turned and strode from

the room. Obi-Wan waited for a few seconds. Then he carefully got up from bed.

"But the Jedi said you're not recovered!" Si Treemba cried in concern.

"Si Treemba," Obi-Wan said slowly, "how big are those thermocoms?"

"Not big." Si Treemba held his hands up eight centimeters apart. "Not hard to conceal."

"If we find those thermocoms, then we'll know who did it," Obi-Wan asserted.

"That's true, Obi-Wan," Si Treemba agreed. Then he stopped and made the same odd hissing sound again. "We are sorry. But when you say 'we' —"

"I mean you and me," Obi-Wan said.

"Ah," Si Treemba said. His greenish skin seemed to pale. "We would have to go to the Offworld side of the ship."

"I know," Obi-Wan said quietly. He knew the risk. And Qui-Gon had ordered him not to. But he was not Qui-Gon's apprentice. He was not honor-bound to obey him.

No doubt Qui-Gon thought him unworthy of the task ahead. But Qui-Gon's hesitations paled next to the Jedi principles. Justice must be sought out.

"Si Treemba, Clat'Ha has great courage," Obi-Wan explained. "But Jemba has power on his side. He is ruthless as well as cunning, and he will stop at nothing. Therefore, he has to be stopped. It's as simple — and as difficult — as that. I understand if you don't wish to help. Truly. We will still be friends."

Si Treemba swallowed. "We will follow you, Obi-Wan," he said.

CHAPTER 9

Obi-Wan's sense of purpose made him feel strong again. He and Si Treemba decided to search the Arconan half of the the *Monument*. It made sense to be able to eliminate the easiest task first.

Obi-Wan and Si Treemba were able to search the kitchens, storage rooms, exercise rooms, and lounges without looking suspicious. Obi-Wan even had Si Treemba lower him down the garbage chutes. They found no sign of the stolen thermocoms.

"We have to search the cabins, Si Treemba," Obi-Wan said, picking a stray piece of garbage from his hair. He sighed. Over four hundred Arconan miners were in those cabins. He couldn't imagine that they would let him just search their rooms.

"That will be no problem, Obi-Wan," Si Treemba replied.

Obi-Wan had forgotten how Arconans think. They had no words for *me* or *mine*. So Si Treemba wandered from cabin to cabin, searching each bunk and storage compartment. A dozen times, Arconans asked, "What are we doing?"

Each time, Si Treemba would merely answer, "We are looking for something that was lost."

To which the Arconan would ask, "May we help find it?"

And Si Treemba would answer, "We need no assistance." Then Si Treemba and Obi-Wan would search the room and leave.

But not all the workers for Arcona Mineral Harvest were Arconan. Some were short, silver-haired Meerians returning to Bandomeer, some Human. Obi-Wan had to treat these carefully. More than once he found himself using the Force to convince some burly miner to let him search.

It was exhausting work for someone who was still recovering, but Obi-Wan ignored his own pain and weariness. A Jedi did not give into such feelings.

After a long day, Obi-Wan and Si Treemba went to the kitchens for a late meal. Obi-Wan ate a full dinner of roast gorak bird cooked in malla petals from Alderaan. Si ate Arconan fungi covered with *dactyl,* a type of yellow ammonia crystal. The Arconan's food smelled . . . well, the fungus wasn't bad, but the dactyl smelled like poison.

Obi-Wan wrinkled his nose. "How could anyone eat that stuff?"

Si Treemba smiled. His faceted eyes glittered. "Some creatures wonder how Humans can drink water, yet you take delight in it. Dactyl is as necessary to us as water is to you." Having said that, he took a couple of crunchy yellow stones and popped them in his mouth like candy.

When Obi-Wan reached for some salt, Si Treemba pulled his own plate away in fear.

"Salt increases our need for dactyl a hundredfold," Si Treemba explained. "It is a very dangerous substance to Arconans."

Obi-Wan sprinkled the salt on his gorak bird. "We all have our own poisons, I guess," he said cheerfully, taking a bite.

Si Treemba grinned at him and crunched on his dactyl. It was almost like being back at the Temple eating with Bant or Reeft, Obi-Wan thought. He missed his friends, but he liked Si Treemba more and more as he spent time with him. The Arconan had a courage and determination that impressed him. And Obi-Wan was aware that it took nerve for an Arconan to break off from the group and help a stranger.

"You know," Obi-Wan remarked, "there's one thing I don't understand. Jemba puts on a good show. But I sense that he's afraid of Clat'Ha and the Arconans."

Si Treemba swallowed his mouthful of dactyl and fungi. "We think you're right, Obi-Wan. He fears us. Even though it is not our intent, he knows that we will destroy him."

"How is that?" Obi-Wan asked.

"In Offworld Mining, the chiefs and overseers make fortunes, while the common workers make nothing. Many of them are slaves. But at Arcona Mineral Harvest, we have no chieftains, no overseers. Each worker shares in the profits. This did not bother Offworld until Clat'Ha became our chief operations manager. She wants to expand our operations. So she contacts the better workers at Offworld. If they are slaves, she offers to buy them and set them free if they will work for us. If they have signed work contracts, she offers to buy the contracts."

"That sounds fair," Obi-Wan said.

"It *is* fair," Si Treemba agreed. "That is exactly why Jemba fears us. Many good workers wish to join us. As good workers join, only the bad will stay at Offworld."

"I see," Obi-Wan said. "So in a few years, Jemba will have only chiefs, with no one to boss around. He'd hate that."

Si Treemba grinned, then turned serious. "But Jemba has stalled us. He has raised the price on labor contracts and slaves. We can no longer afford to hire Offworld workers."

Obi-Wan was beginning to see that the galaxy was a far more complicated place than he'd realized. The Temple had prepared him for so many things. But they had not prepared him for this. He had known that most worlds in the galaxy had outlawed slavery, and he had assumed that it was rare. But here were hundreds of workers locked in an illegal practice.

Obi-Wan was horrified at the idea of slavery. Since Offworld had paid good money to buy and train slaves, the company wasn't likely to sell them cheap — or to let them go without a fight. Clat'Ha had been right when she told Obi-Wan that he had stepped into a war. This battle would probably rage through mining camps on hundreds of worlds.

He wanted to race to the other side of the ship, lightsaber in hand, and right every wrong. But that wasn't the way, he knew. He had to find those thermocoms. Exposure was the only way to fight Jemba.

He pushed his plate away. "We've searched everywhere on this side of the ship, Si," he said. "The thermocoms must be in Offworld territory."

The Arconan boy took a deep breath, then released it slowly. "Good. We are pleased."

"Pleased?" Obi-Wan asked. "But now we have to invade Offworld territory. I thought you were terrified of Hutts."

"That we are," Si Treemba agreed. "But still, we are pleased because if the thermocoms are not here, it means that we are innocent. Someone at Offworld Mining is really trying to kill us."

"Yes, I can see how that would be comforting," Obi-Wan teased, though he did understand. The Arconans were hatched from eggs and raised in a huge nest — with hundreds of brothers and sisters growing together at a time. From their youth, they were trained to think of themselves as a group. The thought that any Arconan — any of Si's brothers or sisters — would do something that might hurt or shame the group must have filled the young Arconan with dread.

"So are you ready to search in Hutt territory?" Obi-Wan asked. "We'll have to find a way to sneak over."

Si Treemba pushed away his plate of fungi and dactyl. "As we said before, Obi-Wan, we will follow you."

Obi-Wan grinned. "You might be sorry you said that."

CHAPTER 10

Obi-Wan and Si Treemba crawled forward through the air shaft and gazed through a grate down into a dark cabin. A huge Whiphid was lying asleep on a bunk, a ball of sour-smelling fur. The odor of cheap Dresselian beer filled the room.

This cabin looked like a monument to filth, just like all the others Obi-Wan had seen today. The Whiphid wore dirty, half-cured hides from his homeworld of Toola. Piles of painted animal skulls were stacked in every corner, looking like hunting trophies. Worse than that, Obi-Wan could see that Hutts had been bunking in the same room: The floor was littered with the furry parts of half-eaten small animals.

Obi-Wan studied the shadowy scene below for a long minute. The Whiphid was probably drunk. Otherwise he would have been out playing sabacc or some other card game with his friends.

But something *felt* wrong. Maybe the Whiphid was only faking sleep. It could be a trap.

Obi-Wan tried to peer farther into the room. It looked empty but for the lone Whiphid. He couldn't see the corners of the room, however.

His unease deepened. He could feel dark ripples in the Force, but what did it mean? Evil streamed through this side of the ship like poisonous air. He'd searched several rooms already. He'd found illegal weapons — riot guns and biotic grenades. He'd found a small casket filled with credit chips that might have been stolen loot. But he hadn't found any thermocoms.

He studied the Whiphid again. He was lying on his cot. Beneath his head Obi-Wan could see a barely concealed weapon. Among such creatures, sleeping with a blaster was the norm.

Obi-Wan watched the Whiphid breathe. He took shallow breaths, a bit too unevenly for Obi-Wan to be comfortable. If he was asleep at all, he was sleeping lightly.

Too often in the past, Obi-Wan's impatience had gotten him into trouble. This time he decided to trust his instincts.

Carefully, quietly, Obi-Wan scooted past this

room. He glanced back behind him in the cramped air duct. Si Treemba was at his heels. The poor Arconan could hardly move his huge triangular head through the shaft.

Then Si Treemba banged his head on the metal duct. It made a small thump. Obi-Wan cringed.

Because Si Treemba's people had evolved in the tunnels of Arcona, his marvelous faceted eyes gave off a faint bioluminescent light. Obviously, Arconans were not animal hunters. Obi-Wan only hoped that as they passed the cabin below, the Whiphid would not glance up and see the Arconan.

Obi-Wan held his breath and moved forward, inching along toward the air vent for the next cabin.

The odor coming from the room ahead was horrible — a mixture of sour fat and greasy hair. Obi-Wan could hear voices, the booming laughter of Hutts, the animal growls of Whiphids.

He brushed aside some dust and peered through the next vent. The cabin was full of Hutts and Whiphids, all crouched around the floor, playing dice.

Si Treemba would never be able to sneak past them. They'd have to back up, as they had done so many times today. Obi-Wan feared they were completely lost.

Glancing back down the air shaft, Obi-Wan could see Si Treemba cautiously inching toward the previous air shaft. Obi-Wan waved a hand, trying to get the Arconan's attention, when suddenly a blinding flash of light erupted through the shaft, and a deafening boom roared.

Someone had shot a blaster through the vent!

Smoke began to fill the air. They were trapped!

Frantically, Obi-Wan signaled at Si Treemba to hurry toward him. But even as he did, a huge furry paw pushed through the metal grate and grabbed Si Treemba by the throat.

Si Treemba's glittering eyes widened in terror. He let out a choked sound that might have been a call for help. Then he was yanked through the grate. Obi-Wan heard the thump of his body hitting the ground.

Through the vent behind him, Obi-Wan heard a Hutt laugh cruelly. "And you said there were womp rats in the air shaft! I told you I smelled an Arconan!"

Obi-Wan's heart pounded. In seconds he knew that someone would stick his head up through the grill, blaster in hand, looking for more like Si Treemba.

Moving as quickly as he dared, he scooted silently toward a corner twenty meters ahead. He pulled himself around it, sweat streaming down his face. Behind him, he heard the faint sound of Si Treemba screaming. A Whiphid roared in anger. Obi-Wan bit his lip. He wanted to block out the sounds of Si Treemba's screams, but he deserved to hear them. He had gotten the Arconan into this mess.

Through the air shaft, he heard someone growl, "I don't see anyone else up here."

He didn't dare return for Si Treemba. Instead, Obi-Wan crawled forward blindly, turning several corners and moving quickly through the ducts. He had to get help!

At last he stopped, panting. There was no help on this side of the ship.

Qui-Gon had warned him to stay out of Offworld territory. Now Obi-Wan realized he had to go back. The Hutts and Whiphids would think Si Treemba was a spy. They might try to torture a confession from him. They might even kill him. And they wouldn't wait long.

He had been so foolish! He should have realized how difficult it would be to penetrate this side of the ship. He had led Si Treemba straight into danger. He had taken advantage of Si Treemba's loyalty to him.

Maybe Qui-Gon's hesitation about him had been right all along. Maybe he didn't deserve to be a Jedi.

Obi-Wan wiped the sweat from his eyes with the hem of his tunic. He made sure his light-saber was holstered securely.

Then he turned back to help his friend.

CHAPTER 11

Qui-Gon swung his legs over his sleep-couch. He felt his heart pound in his chest, every muscle on alert. But why?

He had been resting when he had sensed it. It felt as though danger was near, but Qui-Gon was not in danger . . .

Suddenly, he recognized the feeling. He had experienced it before. Jedi sometimes sense when another Jedi, close to them, is in trouble. At times, they can even see a vague picture of what that trouble might be. Qui-Gon searched his mind, but did not see anything clear. Only haze.

"Obi-Wan," he murmured. It had to be the boy. Qui-Gon fought against the feeling. It was ridiculous, absurd. The boy was not his Padawan. Why would there be such a strong connection between them?

Yet there it was. Yoda would be pleased.

Qui-Gon groaned. He was not.

Wherever he turned, the boy appeared. He was happy to treat Obi-Wan's injuries, but he refused to be responsible for his welfare. If the boy had gotten himself into some sort of mess, he would just have to find his own way out of it.

Qui-Gon stretched out on the sleep-couch again. But this time, although he could quiet his body, he could not quiet his mind.

Time seemed to crawl as Obi-Wan desperately searched for Si Treemba. He had to drag himself through the air shaft, sneaking past miner cabins and peering through grates, holding his breath. Grime covered his hands and grit flew into his eyes and mouth as he stirred up years of dust.

At last he found Si Treemba, four floors down near the belly of the ship. A small cabin had been made into a makeshift prison cell. Apparently, the *Monument* had need of a temporary jail during its transport runs. Considering the crowd on this one, Obi-Wan wasn't surprised.

Obi-Wan peered down through the vent. Si Treemba was chained to the wall by one ankle. He lay sprawled on the floor, his arms outstretched. Just out of his reach lay some yellow crystals of dactyl. Only a half-dozen paces away, a Hutt and two Whiphid guards played cards at a massive carved metal table.

The Arconan boy looked beaten and bruised, but more seemed to be wrong with him than a mere beating. His color had gone from a healthy gray-green to a muddy tan. Obi-Wan could see that the life force in the Arconan was weak, and fading. But why? Si Treemba had ingested his dactyl supply before they'd begun the search. Why had he weakened so fast?

The Hutt slithered over to Si Treemba and grinned as he stared down at the captive. Obi-Wan recognized him. It was the Hutt who had beaten him up the day before.

"Ready to talk yet?" the Hutt asked. "Don't you want that dactyl? I could push a few crystals over."

Si Treemba stared at him silently. Even from above, Obi-Wan could see that his friend's contempt for the Hutt could not mask his fear.

The Hutt leaned closer, his huge head bobbing in front of Si Treemba. "What were you doing in our vents? Who sent you to spy on us?"

Weakly, Si Treemba shook his head.

"You don't look so good," the Hutt sneered. "We gave you enough salt in that saline injection to deplete all the dactyl in your body." He leaned back again and chortled. "So why don't you tell us what we want to know? It beats dying. Someone was with you. Who was it? Arconans never travel alone."

Si Treemba shook his head again. His head lolled back, and his cheek hit the floor.

Frustration filled Obi-Wan. He had to do something. He grasped the vent and pulled it out. He shoved himself into the opening, then somersaulted down to the floor. In a heartbeat, his lightsaber was in his hand.

"Do you only pick on the weak and unarmed, Hutt?" he asked.

For a moment, the Hutt was so astonished that he could only blink at Obi-Wan. Then he began to laugh.

"Blast him," he said offhandedly to the Whiphid guards.

Obi-Wan had counted on the slow reaction time of the Whiphids. They stared at him, their mouths open underneath their tusks.

Obi-Wan sprang forward, slashing at the heavy table. The lightsaber cut through the thick legs easily. With a crash, the table thudded down on the Whiphids. The flimsy stools they had been sitting on collapsed under the weight, pinning them to the floor. They howled in surprise and pain.

"Sorry to break up your game," Obi-Wan said. Keeping his eye on the surprised Hutt, he reached over to the table and grabbed the key to Si Treemba's leg cuff. The shackle was an ancient thing of metal, with a simple lock. Obi-Wan tossed the key to Si Treemba.

The Hutt slithered toward him. "So, young Jedi, you have not yet learned your lesson? How dare you defy me, the mighty Grelb!"

"Oh, but I did learn something," Obi-Wan said. He held the lightsaber in readiness. "You prey on the weak. Now I am prepared to fight you, coward."

Grelb eyed the lightsaber with contempt. "With that?"

Obi-Wan glanced behind the Hutt at Si Treemba. The Arconan had managed to free himself. He was quickly eating up all the dactyl on the floor. Already, his color was starting to brighten.

As the Hutt moved toward Obi-Wan, his enormous fists raised, Obi-Wan ducked and rolled in a classic Jedi defense maneuver. As he passed, he delivered a lightsaber blow to the Hutt's flank. He heard the flesh sizzle.

Grelb roared in fury as he staggered back. His enormous bulk made him clumsy, and he fell onto the table, crushing the Whiphid's legs even more. They howled in pain and beat against him with their fists.

"Hurry, Si," Obi-Wan urged. Keeping himself

between Grelb and Si Treemba, he waited until the Arconan had reached the door. Then he hurried after him as Grelb tried to struggle to rise. Hutts were powerful, but they were not exactly light on their feet.

"You won't get away with this, Jedi!" Grelb bellowed. "That Arconan is a spy! This is war!"

Obi-Wan ignored him. He half-dragged Si Treemba down the hallway. Lucky for them, the lower level wasn't well-trafficked. They were able to reach the Arconan boundary without any more encounters.

As they crossed onto the Arconan side of the ship, Obi-Wan saw two Arconan border guards hurry away. He knew they were going to alert Clat'Ha that the two had returned — and had come from Offworld territory.

That meant, of course, that Qui-Gon would discover that Obi-Wan had disobeyed his order.

Si Treemba stopped. He turned to Obi-Wan, his luminous eyes glittering once again with the same warm light. "We thank you, Obi Wan. We owe our lives to you."

"You owe your capture to me, too," Obi-Wan answered ruefully. "I'm sorry, Si Treemba."

"But once again your courage saved us," Si Treemba said, grasping his shoulder.

"What about *your* courage?" Obi-Wan countered. "Think about it, Si Treemba. You were dying, and you still would not betray me. You just faced down a Hutt!"

A slow smile spread over Si Treemba's face. "So we did," he said, pleased. "So we did."

"Don't get too cocky," Obi-Wan said with a sigh. "We still have to face Clat'Ha and Qui-Gon. They aren't going to be happy about this."

As soon as Obi-Wan Kenobi and Si Treemba were gone, Grelb slithered to Jemba and told him everything.

The great gray Hutt loomed over Grelb, gasping in rage. Jemba was hundreds of years older than Grelb, and also much larger. "So," Jemba growled, looking around his stateroom in a rage. "I knew it. The Jedi Knight and his young pupil have joined with the Arconans against me!"

"It was inevitable, O Great One," Grelb said. "They do not like our kind."

"It's *your* fault!" Jemba said. "I should chop off your tail for this and have it for dinner."

Grelb's hearts began racing in fear, and he immediately coiled his tail up near his body.

Jemba continued, "If you were going to sabotage the tunnelers, you should have waited until we got to Bandomeer."

Grelb tried to look hurt by the accusation, but Jemba did not fall for it. The huge Hutt slapped

Grelb's face hard enough so that Grelb felt as if his brains had turned to jelly.

After picking himself up off the floor, Grelb said, "You've never complained about my methods before!" Theft, sabotage, and murder were Grelb's methods, but he made sure that Offworld Mining always profited by them.

"But this time there are Jedi around!" Jemba roared.

"I did not know that the boy was a Jedi when I gave him his first beating," Grelb apologized. "If I had, he'd be dead by now. I promise, next time —"

Jemba pointed a huge finger at Grelb. "The boy is onto your schemes. There won't be a next time. Let me handle this!"

"As you please," Grelb said. He turned away and slithered from the room. As the door hissed closed behind him, Grelb clenched his fists, imagining that he was squeezing the throat of Obi-Wan Kenobi.

Of course there will be a next time, Grelb promised himself.

CHAPTER 12

Obi-Wan considered retiring to his cabin, but he knew he'd rather face Qui-Gon sooner than later. He suggested that Si Treemba get some rest, but the Arconan refused.

"We will face them together," Si Treemba said, drawing himself up to his full height.

They found the Jedi and Clat'Ha in the Arconans' lounge, where the lights were always turned low to simulate night and the music droids softly played Arconan flutes. Few Arconans were in the lounge so late. The few that were there had their eyes closed, and stood as still as statues — the Arconan equivalent of sleep.

Qui-Gon stood at a bar, drinking some bluish juice. Clat'Ha stood near him, an untouched glass of juice sat in front of her on the bar. One look at them and Obi-Wan knew they both were aware of what had happened on the Offworld side of the ship.

"At least you're still in one piece this time," Qui-Gon said, eyeing him coldly. "Well, did you discover anything?"

"No," Obi-Wan admitted. "Si Treemba was captured before we could find the thermo-coms."

"Obi-Wan rescued us," Si Treemba praised. "We were shackled to the floor, and he stood up to Grelb the Hutt by himself —"

"A man who puts himself in the path of danger deserves to face it alone," Qui-Gon said sternly.

Obviously, Obi-Wan's bravery did not impress him. Si Treemba quieted, shooting a look at Obi-Wan that said *we tried.*

"You deliberately disobeyed my order," Qui-Gon said evenly.

"With respect, I am not under your charge, Qui-Gon Jinn," Obi-Wan said quietly. "As you keep reminding me."

Qui-Gon turned to him and stared for a moment. Obi-Wan couldn't read what was behind that keen blue gaze. At last, he spoke. "Your meddling has only made things worse."

"I made matters worse?" Obi-Wan asked. "What do you mean?"

"Yes, you have," Qui-Gon said. His face remained impassive, his tone neutral. But now Obi-Wan could sense his deep irritation. He had hoped to win the Jedi's respect. Instead, he was looked at as a pest, not even worthy of great anger. "You sneaked into Offworld territory, invaded their privacy, got caught, and had to fight your way out again. They will surely retaliate."

"But it was worth the risk," Obi-Wan tried. "If we had found the thermocoms —"

Clat'Ha interrupted him. "The thermocoms were found an hour ago, hidden in a barrel of lubricant. Whoever dropped them in there didn't expect them to be found."

Obi-Wan's mouth snapped shut. Qui-Gon was right. He had risked the fragile peace on the ship for nothing.

"Can't you see that this isn't about thermocoms?" Qui-Gon said, trying to keep his voice even. "A Jedi must look at the larger picture. The reason for my order was because I wanted tensions to cool. I wanted to engender trust. How can the Offworlders trust the Jedi, if they find you sneaking around their territory? How can —"

The room suddenly shook, and there was a rumbling boom. Qui-Gon's drink went sliding from the bar, and the cup crashed to the floor. Si Treemba pitched onto his belly. Warning sirens began to wail.

"What hit us?" Clat'Ha shouted.

But Obi-Wan knew that if they'd collided with

another ship, or an asteroid, in hyperspace, it would have torn the ship apart. Distantly, Obi-Wan heard the *whunk whunk whunk* of the ship's guns firing.

Qui-Gon strode to the window. His hand rested on his lightsaber. "Pirates," he announced.

CHAPTER 13

Qui-Gon raced for the bridge, down the main corridors. Obi-Wan, Si Treemba, and Clat'Ha followed at a dead run. All around the ship, Arconans were whining in terror — making the strange hissing sound of their kind. They backed into their rooms and locked their doors.

Through the grates under the floor Qui-Gon could hear the grind of generators charging the ship's shields. Meanwhile, the steady *whunk whunk* sound continued as blasters fired.

He thought he knew what had happened. Pirates sometimes mined the shipping lanes. When the ship hit a mine, the hyperdrive blew, and the ship would drop back out of hyperspace.

As it did, the pirates would open fire, destroying the ship's weapons and engines so swiftly that unwary travelers seldom had time to react.

Then the pirates would send boarding parties out to strip anything they could from their victims.

A miner transport like the *Monument* didn't have much worth stealing, but the pirates wouldn't know that — not until they'd blown it to pieces and searched through the rubble.

The floor shuddered under the impact of another explosion. As the ship twisted to its side, Qui-Gon rounded a corner. Ahead was a transparisteel view port. Through it, he could see five Togorian warships, all shaped like red birds of prey. Two screamed past his port. Green bolts of blaster fire erupted from the warships, slamming into the *Monument*. Metal shrieked in protest. The corridors filled with greasy smoke.

The *Monument*'s guns had gone silent. Now, Qui-Gon could see why — the gun turrets had been blown away. Bits of burning slag lit up like glowing stars where the turrets had once stood.

The *Monument* floated dead in space. Though fire alarms sounded, no one on the bridge was shouting orders. Now a Togorian cruiser raced toward the ship.

Qui-Gon stood, watching helplessly as the cruiser approached. There were times when he wished that he was not alone, times when he wished that he had not lost his last Padawan, Xanatos.

"Obi-Wan," Qui-Gon called. Even though he did not fully trust the boy, he didn't see any other choice. They needed some kind of plan, and they all had to work together if they hoped to survive. "The pirates are getting ready to board," he said crisply. "I'll try to stop them. Go to the bridge and see if the crew is alive. If they are not, I want you to pilot this ship out of here."

Qui-Gon stared hard at the boy. He was asking a lot, he knew. He knew that as a Jedi student, Obi-Wan had flown a few ships in simulation, and most likely piloted some cloud cars around Coruscant. But he'd never piloted a ship like this, and he'd never been in battle.

"I can fight alongside you," Obi-Wan protested.

Qui-Gon turned and grasped the boy by both elbows. "Listen to me. You must obey this time. Trust my judgment. I can hold back the pirates, but we'll all die if the ship remains dead in space. Don't worry about where to go. Just fly anywhere. Once the pirates start boarding, their friends won't be able to fire on us for fear of killing their leaders. Go now. Fly."

Obi-Wan nodded. Qui-Gon could see the un-certainty in the boy's eyes. Qui-Gon wasn't sure if Obi-Wan would be able to pilot the ship, either.

But then again, he wasn't sure he himself could hold off the pirates.

Obi-Wan nodded. "I won't let you down."

Qui-Gon watched as Obi-Wan sprinted to-ward the bridge with Si Treemba behind him. Suddenly, the boy looked so young. . . .

For half a moment, Qui-Gon was tempted to follow him and leave the pirates to the Whiphids and Arconans. But the miners wouldn't be a match for the Togorians. He would have to trust Obi-Wan.

Qui-Gon heard the distant roar of small blasters. That could mean only one thing: the pirates had already boarded. Though the Arco-nans were choosing to hide from the battle, the Offworld miners were putting up a fight.

Of course, the pirates would send more than one boarding party. Qui-Gon decided to let the Offworlders protect themselves. He dashed down a side corridor, toward the docking bay. Clat'Ha ran behind him.

He rounded a corner. A huge Togorian pirate stood directly in his path, his eyes flashing like green embers in the dark fur of his face. The Togorian reached out with his enormous claws to rake Qui-Gon.

But Qui-Gon was a Jedi Master. The Force had already warned him. He twisted under the pirate's arms, anticipating the move, and grasped the lightsaber attached to his belt. The blade came up cleanly, slicing the Togorian at the knees. The Togorian roared in pain.

Behind the fallen pirate, more Togorians rounded a corner and ran toward them. Clat'Ha, in a blind panic, pulled her own blaster and opened fire. One Togorian screamed in pain, its huge fangs gaping and showing blood.

All of the Togorians returned fire with their own blasters. Qui-Gon dodged two bolts, then used his lightsaber to deflect three more.

Clat'Ha dropped low, screaming in rage. She was an able warrior, but they were outnumbered twenty to one. Qui-Gon vowed to do his best to keep her alive.

The door to the bridge was sealed shut, and burning hot. Obi-Wan could feel heat radiating from it as he tried to open it. A fire raged on the other side. Ignoring the pain, he tried to wedge his fingers in the crack to pull it open.

"It's no use," Si Treemba told him. "That's a fire door. It locks if the bridge is burning."

Obi-Wan backed from the door. The bridge must have taken a direct hit from one of the To-gorian ships. But a hit from a heavy blaster or a proton torpedo would have done more than just start a fire. Most likely it had punched a hole in the hull.

It would be dangerous to try to open the door. There *might* only be a fire, but it could be worse. All of the air could have escaped from the room.

He remembered the look on Qui-Gon's face as the Jedi Master asked for his help. He couldn't let him down this time.

Carefully, Obi-Wan struggled to calm himself, to use the Force. He could sense the latching mechanism, and it would only take a little effort to move it.

But then what? If he opened it, he could get pulled into space. Or toxic smoke could roil into the corridor and suffocate him, or the fire might spread into the halls.

He didn't have a choice. He focused his attention, and the door slid open.

Immediately, a stiff wind knocked him in the back. The breath left Obi-Wan's lungs, and the ship's air whisked past him, sucked into the vacuum of space. Obi-Wan grabbed the door-frame to keep from getting sucked out. It was all that he could do to hold on. Behind him, Si

Treemba got a handhold on the edge of a control box.

The bridge had indeed been hit. Air screamed out through a small round hole up above the view port.

"I have to plug the hole!" Obi-Wan shouted to Si Treemba.

But before Obi-Wan could move, Si Treemba dropped to the floor. He crawled across the bridge, reaching for handhold after handhold. Obi-Wan could only hang on to the door frame and watch. He couldn't stop Si Treemba, and he couldn't help him.

Si Treemba reached for a spherical compass — the round metal object that served as a backup in case the main nav computer was hit or disabled. Fighting the screaming wind, Si Treemba stumbled to the hull and released the compass near the hole. The vaccum sucked it in, and immediately the rushing air quieted.

"Good work!" Obi-Wan called as he ran to the pilot console. The captain and his copilot were still strapped into their seats, drowsy from loss of air. In another minute, they'd have suffocated. As it was, both men were unconscious. The room felt hot. Blaster fire had ripped through the navigation terminal, and metal slag pooled everywhere. But with so little air in the room, the fires had gone out.

Obi-Wan unbuckled the captain and moved him onto the floor. Then he looked at the control panel. There were so many lights and buttons. For a moment he was stunned, unsure what to do.

He looked up at the view port.

Togorian warships surrounded the *Monument*. A heavy cruiser that had been refitted as a gun ship edged nearer. Its shields had to be down for it to be so close.

A red light blinked insistently on Obi-Wan's console. In a daze he realized that the forward proton torpedo tubes were loaded and armed. They were standard defensive gear for transports traveling in such a region. His targeting computer was down, but he aimed for the bridge of the gun ship without it.

His heart pounded. He was afraid of what he had to do. He hoped that Qui-Gon was right, that the pirates wouldn't dare to fire back with their own men aboard. Because if they did fire back, they'd hit with everything they had.

"What are you going to do, Obi-Wan?" Si Treemba asked, holding on to the bridge console.

"Send a message to the Togorians," Obi-Wan answered grimly. "We're not dead yet!"

Reaching across the console, he launched the proton torpedoes.

Blaster fire lit the smoky corridors of the *Monument*, blinding him. Qui-Gon deflected and dodged the bolts.

Dead Togorians were strewn in the hall behind. Live Togorians choked the hall ahead. Their roaring resounded from the walls.

For a moment, he was pinned behind the dead. He wished that he had some backup. But the Offworlders were fighting on another front.

"Where are your Arconans?" he shouted to Clat'Ha. "We could use some help."

"Arconans don't fight!" Clat'Ha shouted back as she snapped a shot at a Togorian. "They probably locked themselves in their rooms!"

"What about Jemba's men?" Qui-Gon asked. "Maybe you should contact them for help!"

"They wouldn't come," Clat'Ha said grimly. "I'm afraid it's you and me, Qui-Gon."

A Togorian pirate captain lunged down the corridor, bursting through the screen of smoke. He was huge, nearly twice as tall as a man. His black body armor was scarred and pitted from a thousand fights. A Human skull dangled from a chain around his neck. His fur was as dark as night, and his green eyes gleamed wickedly.

He carried a huge vibro-ax in one hand, an energy shield in the other. The pirate's pointed ears were drawn back flat against his skull. He stepped forward to meet it.

"Meet your death, Jedi!" the Togorian pirate roared. "I have hunted your kind before, and I will gnaw your bones tonight!"

Suddenly, Qui-Gon realized that the pirates behind their dark captain were retreating, back toward the hold. There was nowhere to go back there, except another access tunnel. The pirates were probably trying to circle behind him.

Clat'Ha rushed forward and fired her blaster. The Togorian raised his shield against it, deflecting it easily. Then he raised his deadly vibro-ax. With only the slightest touch, the weapon could sever a man's head. Qui-Gon moved forward in one flowing movement, his lightsaber held high.

"No doubt you have killed before," Qui-Gon said softly. "But you shall not be gnawing any bones tonight."

He leaped at the Togorian pirate. The pirate roared and swung his ax.

A blinding flash as bright as a solar flare lit space as the proton torpedoes struck the Togorian gun ship.

Obi-Wan shielded his eyes from the intense light. Si Treemba cried out.

Half of the gun ship disintegrated, hurtling debris into space. A second blast followed the first, as the gun ship's arsenal exploded.

Bits of metal riddled the *Monument*. A huge section of the blown gun ship hurtled into a second Togorian warship.

Obi-Wan didn't plan to wait and see if the pirates would shoot him down. While they recovered, he hit a button, loading more torpedoes into his launch tube.

With the navigation console out, the only way to fly the ship was manually. Obi-Wan grabbed the control, pulled back hard, and hit the thrusters. He heard the harsh sound of metal rending. Had he just ruined the engines?

Quickly, he consulted the display terminals. He saw the source of the sound. Two Togorian cruisers were latched to his docking bays. By blasting off, Obi-Wan was ripping away from the ships — tearing apart the seals to the doors.

All the air by the docking bays would rush into space.

Qui-Gon had gone to stop the pirates' boarding party.

Obi-Wan gritted his teeth and fervently hoped that only pirates would be swept out into space with the wreckage.

Ahead of him, a Togorian warship opened fire.

* * *

The floor lurched under Qui-Gon's feet as he met the pirate captain. The huge Togorian weighed four times as much as a man.

Even under normal circumstances, it would have been all that Qui-Gon could do to fend off the pirate. He tried to catch his footing as he blocked the monster's blow.

The pirate almost fell, but recovered in time to raise the vibro-ax. The blade bit deep into Qui-Gon's right shoulder, driving him to the floor.

Qui-Gon gasped from the searing pain. His shoulder burned as if it were on fire. He tried to lift his arm, but it was useless.

Behind the pirate, Qui-Gon heard the sound of peeling metal. The seals to the hold had ripped apart. Wind howled down the hall as the ship's air screamed away. Qui-Gon saw droplets of his own blood stripped away like rain in a storm.

Debris came hurtling down the hall — blasters and helmets of dead Togorians. They battered the huge Togorian pirate, and he raised his shield, fighting forward, pressing the attack.

Qui-Gon let the wind pull him, so that he slid along the floor toward the vacuum of space, closer to the pirate captain.

If he died, he would take the monster with him.

*　　*　　*

Heavy blaster fire ripped through the hull of the *Monument*. The Togorian warship had taken aim at the bridge, but with the sudden thrust of the huge ship, the blaster bolts had struck the ship behind their mark.

Obi-Wan pushed away the thought of who might have died in that attack. He reversed thrusters.

The warship's next salvo fell short, blasting harmlessly into space. Obi-Wan took half a moment to aim his proton torpedoes, then launched them down the warship's gullet.

As he was sucked toward the space vacuum, Qui-Gon called his lightsaber to his left hand. He aimed a blow at the pirate captain's feet. The Togorian grabbed a handhold and leaped high, evading the cut, then landed directly on Qui-Gon's left arm with his booted feet.

Fighting the pain, Qui-Gon tried to bring up his lightsaber, but the huge Togorian had him pinned. Qui-Gon twisted desperately, but he couldn't get away. With his left arm pinned and his right arm badly wounded Qui-Gon could do little to fight the monster.

The pirate captain roared madly in triumph, and the wind seemed to roar with him. It tore down the corridors like a tornado. Qui-Gon could hardly breathe.

Suddenly the pirate's head disappeared. The huge Togorian hurtled backward, grabbed by the fury of the wind.

Qui-Gon looked up the hall. Clat'Ha crouched on the floor, desperately clinging to the handle of a locker door with one hand, her heavy blaster in the other.

In the heat of the battle, the Togorian pirate had forgotten about the woman.

Down the hall was a bulkhead door that should have closed automatically when the air pressure dropped. But with all the damage to the ship, it was no surprise that it hadn't worked.

Qui-Gon was bleeding badly, and could hardly breathe. Weakly, with the last of his will, he reached out with the Force and moved a bit of debris, touching the controls to the door and sliding it closed. As the wind stopped screaming through the ship, everything became deathly silent.

All that Qui-Gon could hear was his own heart beating, and Clat'Ha gasping for air.

The Togorian warship exploded in a burst of light.

Si Treemba worked at the communications console, launching distress beacons. It might take days for a Republic ship to respond, or one could arrive in a matter of seconds. It was impossible to know who would be traveling the space lanes.

Suddenly the Togorian warships peeled away from the *Monument*. Their gun ship and warship were destroyed. Their captain's cruiser and a second boarding vessel had ripped away from the *Monument*'s hull, and dead pirates could be seen littering space.

The last of the pirates blasted off into hyperspace, never guessing that they'd been bested by a twelve-year-old boy.

Obi-Wan piloted the *Monument* among the glimmering stars. Warning claxons were ringing everywhere. Monitors showed air leaking from a dozen holes.

"It looks like the ship is falling apart," Obi-Wan said to Si Treemba.

Si Treemba nodded his triangular head worriedly. "We have to land now, Obi-Wan."

"Land where?" Obi-Wan asked, looking ahead at nothing but empty space.

Si Treemba bent over the nav computer. "It's not working," he said.

"I know," Obi-Wan replied. "That's why I'm flying manually. Where are the crew? Why isn't anyone coming to help us?"

"They're probably dealing with the wounded, or maybe they are wounded themselves." Si Treemba peered ahead through the view screen. "Wait! There!"

Obi-Wan could just glimpse the planet ahead, a blue marble the color of water, shot through with the white of clouds.

"How do we know we can breathe the air?" Obi-Wan asked. The atmosphere might be poison, the planet hostile.

"It has got to be better than breathing in a vacuum," Si Treemba suggested.

The Arconan's faceted eyes met Obi-Wan's. The great ship shuddered, and another warning monitor went off, signaling that air pressure was dropping.

"We don't think we have a choice," Si Treemba said softly.

Grelb and his men hurried down the hallways through the Arconan side of the ship. Jemba the Hutt's miners had fought well against the pirates on their side, but dozens of stout Hutts and Whiphids had died.

There was a good chance that the Arconans would be dead, too. Grelb was hoping to steal some loot from the bodies.

But when he reached the doors to the Arconan

hold, he found that the Arconans hadn't fought at all. Instead, they'd let their pet Jedi protect them.

Grelb glanced around a corner and saw the hated Clat'Ha helping Qui-Gon off the floor. The Jedi had a deep wound in his right shoulder, and his left arm was sore and swollen.

The Hutt smiled, and jerked his head back from the corridor before anyone looked his way.

He whispered to the Whiphids at his back. "Go and tell Jemba: the Arconans are all cowards who dared not come out of their rooms to fight. And their precious Jedi looks as if he's barely alive. Now is a good time to strike!"

Obi-Wan flew over a watery world from daylight into darkness, to a night lit by five glowing moons that hung in the sky like multicolored stones. Beneath him, enormous creatures flew in great flocks. They were silvery in the moonlight, with long bullet-shaped bodies and powerful wings. They looked like some strange species of flying fish whose wings had evolved to remarkable size. They stretched their wings wide, half-asleep as they rode the wind. Some of them looked up at his ship curiously.

Clinging to the manual controls, with the ship bucking and rattling, Obi-Wan could see only ocean in every direction. Then, at last, on the

horizon ahead he glimpsed one small rocky island, waves breaking against its shore.

He aimed the ship at the rock, held tight to the
controls, and groaned with effort as he tried to
slow the ship's fall.

CHAPTER 14

Dozens of miners had been killed or injured in the attack, so the sickbay was full. Yet few of those injured were Arconans. As Clat'Ha predicted, all of the Arconans but Si Treemba had locked themselves in their rooms at the first sign of danger. Most of the injuries fell to the ship's crew and to some of Jemba's miners.

Qui-Gon's injuries would have been severe for a common man, but the Jedi waited until others were attended to before requesting the medic droid to bandage him in his room. Clat'Ha refused to leave his side, no matter how he urged her to rest.

"Not until I know you're okay," she told him steadily.

Obi-Wan had landed the ship only a few meters from the rocky beach. Night hung like a mist over the island. After determining the atmosphere was stable, a dozen of the ship's crew had gone outside to begin repairing the damage to the hull, and others were checking the surroundings. The silvery draigons were everywhere, riding the night sky, apparently asleep on the wing. Many of them also perched on the island cliffs. It wasn't safe to stay outside, and the captain said that no one would be allowed to work in the daylight, once the beasts awoke. The ship's engineer reported that it would take two nights to get the ship running.

Obi-Wan reached Qui-Gon's cabin just as the medic droid finished spraying a disinfectant bandage over Qui-Gon's ghastly wound. Then he began to glue the wound closed. The pirate chieftain's vibro-ax had slashed Qui-Gon across the back of his shoulders, down to the ribs. Obi-Wan felt dizzy just looking at the wound, but Qui-Gon sat quietly, letting the droid do his work.

"You're lucky to be alive," the medic droid told Qui-Gon. "But your wounds should heal in time. Are you sure you don't want something to ease the pain?"

"No, I'll be fine," Qui-Gon answered, his voice steady. He turned his gaze to Clat'Ha. "Now will you get some rest?"

She nodded wearily. "I'll check back on you later." Clat'Ha left with the medic droid. The door hissed closed behind them.

Qui-Gon eased himself into a chair. Obi-Wan waited for him to speak or acknowledge his presence.

Qui-Gon's blue gaze studied Obi-Wan keenly for a moment. "Obi-Wan, when you accelerated the ship, what thoughts did you have?"

"Thoughts?" Obi-Wan asked doubtfully. "I wasn't thinking about much of anything. I was afraid of the pirates, and I just knew that I had to get away fast." He was too exhausted to care too much about giving a wrong answer. Better to just speak the blunt truth. Qui-Gon would approve of his actions or not. He was tired of trying to please him.

"So you didn't think about the fact that you would tear their ships from the docking bays and kill hundreds of pirates in the process?" Qui-Gon asked in a neutral tone.

"I didn't have time to think about what I was doing," Obi-Wan replied. "The Force led me."

"Were you frightened? Angry?"

"Both," Obi-Wan admitted. "I . . . fired on the pirates. I killed, but I didn't do it in anger. I did it to save lives."

Qui-Gon nodded, just the smallest of movements. "I see." It was the answer Qui-Gon had been looking for. It demonstrated that Obi-Wan was growing stronger in the ways of the Force.

Yet Qui-Gon felt strangely dissatisfied. He

tested his heart. Had he actually wanted the boy to fail his test? That would be a grave flaw for a Jedi.

But he couldn't help himself. True, Obi-Wan had not let him down. He had bravely accepted the task of piloting the ship. Hundreds of lives had been in his hands, and he had not hesitated. He had done honor to his training.

Why was it so hard for Qui-Gon to trust him still?

Because I trusted another. I trusted Xanatos completely, and disaster was the result.

The sense of loss was so great that even now Qui-Gon felt it like a living wound. He'd rather have taken a dozen blows from the pirate chieftain's vibro-ax than to ever feel such loss and pain again.

Obi-Wan stood before Qui-Gon, confused. He was so tired he was almost weaving on his feet. Had he answered badly or well? He didn't know. All he could sense was a struggle in Qui-Gon that he didn't understand. They had worked together to save the ship. A bond should have formed between them. But Obi-Wan felt they were farther apart than ever.

Should he speak? Perhaps if he asked Qui-Gon what he was thinking, the Jedi would tell him.

But before Obi-Wan could raise his nerve, a

vicious pounding sounded at the door. Obi-Wan hurried to open it.

Si Treemba rushed in. The Arconan was out of breath, panting.

"What's wrong?" Qui-Gon asked. He stood and tenderly stretched his shoulder, to see how well the glue had set.

"Please come quickly," Si Treemba panted. "Jemba the Hutt has stolen our dactyl!"

CHAPTER 15

"You won't get away with this," Qui-Gon warned Jemba the Hutt. He spoke calmly. Behind Qui-Gon, dozens of Arconans stood silent. Obi-Wan stood among them, watching the Jedi's back. Qui-Gon was sorely wounded, and seemed on the verge of collapse.

Jemba shook in amusement like a giant gray worm. "What can you do, puny Jedi?" he boomed gleefully. "No one can stop the great Jemba! Your Arconans were too frightened to face the pirates. They hid, while my men fought and died. Soon these cowards will be my slaves!"

Jemba and his men had taken over the Arconans' lounge. A wall of Offworld miners — Hutts, Whiphids, Humans, and droids — backed Jemba. The Offworlders stood ready for battle. Qui-Gon, Obi-Wan, and the Arconans stared down the barrels of at least thirty blasters. Some of the Offworld thugs also held shields and wore armor. Jemba's men obviously held more than just the Arconans' dactyl. They held most of the ship's weapons.

Obi-Wan felt outraged. Beside him, Clat'Ha was livid. She held her hands down loosely, ready to draw her weapon. But she and the Arconans would be vastly outgunned.

"It is not justice you seek, Jemba," Qui-Gon tried to reason. "You hope only to satisfy your greed. Nothing will be solved this way. Put down your weapons."

Qui-Gon called on the Force, trying to coax the Hutt to stop this madness. But for hours now he'd been focusing on his wound, trying to speed its healing, ignoring his own pain. He was too weak to persuade the Hutt.

Jemba waved a hand, as if testing the air. "Ooh, is that your powerful Force I feel? Ha!" he spat. "Your Jedi tricks are so puny, they make me laugh. They cannot work on the great Jemba. And look at you, Jedi. You don't have the sense to stay out of the way of a vibro-ax. Anyone can see you are too frail to fight. There is nothing you can do to stop me."

Fury filled Obi-Wan at the Hutt's taunting. He leaped past Qui-Gon, directly in front of Jemba.

"*I* can stop you!" he shouted. He brought up his lightsaber.

Jemba's huge eyes narrowed in anger. The thugs who surrounded him held their ground. They weren't afraid of a mere boy.

"What, Jedi?" Jemba said contemptuously to Qui-Gon. "You send a child to fight me? Is this some insult?" Jemba looked to his right and left, and raised a huge fist. If he let it fall, Obi-Wan knew that it would be the signal for his men to open fire. Obi-Wan would not be able to deflect more than a few blaster bolts.

Qui-Gon reached out and touched Obi-Wan's elbow. "Put your lightsaber away," he said calmly. "You can't win like this. If he opens fire, people will die needlessly. A Jedi must know his *true* enemies."

Obi-Wan was shaking. He suddenly felt confused.

"What do you mean?" he asked. Sweat streamed down his face. "Which one of them is our enemy?"

"Anger is our enemy," Qui-Gon said reasonably. He shot a glare across the room to Jemba. "Greed and fear are also our enemies. The Arconans can live without dactyl for awhile. You do not need to fight now. Haste is another enemy."

Obi-Wan saw the wisdom in Qui-Gon's

words. He powered down his lightsaber, bowed to Jemba as if to a worthy opponent, and stepped back.

"A wise move, little one," Jemba said. Then the Hutt broke into a deep laugh. He shouted across the room to the Arconans, "I want workers. And I am willing to pay well."

The Hutt's voice created a small echo. Behind Qui-Gon, Arconans began to mutter restlessly, almost a humming sound.

Clat'Ha shouted, "Offworld doesn't pay its workers well!"

Jemba pounded his chest. "I will pay in food and dactyl!" he said. "For a day of labor, I will give my workers a day of life!"

"You offer to pay these people with dactyl that you stole from them?" Obi-Wan asked. He could not believe what he heard. It was all he could do to restrain from launching himself across the room to hack Jemba to pieces.

Jemba smiled hugely. "Indeed. Those who work for me will live. Those who do not will die. What better pay could I give?"

The Arconans had been talking softly. To Obi-Wan's further amazement, some of them immediately began to stride across the room toward Jemba. More followed. Si Treemba hesitated, then joined them.

"Wait!" Clat'Ha commanded the Arconans. "What are you doing?"

The Arconans stopped and looked back. "We are miners," Si Treemba said. "Whether we live under Jemba, or under another, it matters not."

"But, Si Treemba, what of your freedom?" Obi-Wan asked. "You can't just give it up!"

Si Treemba looked at him sadly. "You are our friend, Obi-Wan. But you do not understand. Humans may value freedom as much as life. But we do not." As a group, the Arconans turned and headed toward Jemba.

Obi-Wan struggled to understand his friend's words. Arconans were hatched in nests where they shared everything. On Arcona, they dug in the soil for deep roots that held water and food. They relied upon one another wholly. Once on Bandomeer, they would mine for Jemba. As long as their community survived, as long as *we* remained, freedom did not matter.

"If you go with him," Clat'Ha warned, "he will take all that he can from you, and give nothing in return except what is already yours by right. Jemba will grow huge, while the Arconans grow weak. Is that what you want?"

"No," Si Treemba admitted. "But we do not wish to die."

"Then you must fight him," Clat'Ha urged. "When you are faced with danger, you build walls and hide behind them. That is the Arconan way. But when a daggerlip tears down your walls, you fight. Jemba is no better than a daggerlip. He intends to destroy us. We can defeat him."

Clat'Ha drew her blaster, and the Offworld miners raised their weapons and shields, prepared to fight. Obi-Wan studied the fiery woman. Her fierceness filled the room. All it needed was a spark to ignite.

It was a battle they were bound to lose. Qui-Gon was right. This was not the time or place to fight. Jemba had to be stopped. They could not stop him here.

"Si Treemba," Obi-Wan called. "Friend. I ask this one thing of you. Wait."

Qui-Gon shot him a look of respect. Obi-Wan did not have time to be pleased by it. He focused all his attention on Si Treemba. Sometimes, the force of friendship could work where the Force could not.

Si Treemba faced him, torn. It would take an act of great courage for him to divide himself from his fellow Arconans, Obi-Wan knew. He waited, knowing that to speak again would be to insult Si Treemba.

Slowly, Si Treemba nodded. Then he moved to the other side of the room to stand with Obi-Wan and Clat'Ha.

A low, anxious hissing filled the room. One by one, the Arconans followed Si Treemba.

CHAPTER 16

The meeting ended in a stalemate. There was nothing left to do but leave. Obi-Wan stayed with Qui-Gon. Although the Jedi held himself erect during the confrontation, sweat beaded his forehead and Obi-Wan could only imagine the concentration it took for him to stay focused.

"I'll see you back to your cabin," Obi-Wan told him. He knew Qui-Gon must be feeling weak when the Jedi didn't try to argue.

By the time Qui-Gon reached the corridor where his cabin was located, his walk was unsteady and his vision clouded. He was grateful for Obi-Wan's presence at his side. As he rounded the last corner, he staggered. Obi-Wan grabbed his arm and held him upright.

"Are you all right?" Obi-Wan asked, his voice thick with concern.

"I will be," Qui-Gon said weakly. "I . . . just need . . . to focus."

Obi-Wan helped him into his cabin and waited until he was seated. A plan had been growing in his mind since the confrontation. This time, he would not make the mistake of failing to inform Qui-Gon.

"Master Jinn," Obi-Wan began. "I have an idea. I will go back into the air vents, into Off-world territory. I know the layout now. I will wait till Jemba is alone and ambush him."

Qui-Gon closed his eyes for a moment, as if Obi-Wan's suggestion had pained him as much as his wound. "No," he said flatly. "You will not."

Just moments ago, he had been impressed by Obi-Wan's handling of the Arconan situation, and how he had backed off from Jemba with dignity. Now the boy was making reckless plans again, letting his eagerness take over his judgment.

Of course, Qui-Gon had to admit, the plans were no more reckless than some of those Qui-Gon had thought up in his own youth. Still, he felt a disappointment so keen that it surprised him. Were his feelings continually to take him unaware when it came to this boy?

Wearily, Qui-Gon raised himself up in the

chair. His shoulder suddenly flamed where the pirate had struck him. He'd been holding that pain at bay, but now it overwhelmed him.

"Look, you're wounded," Obi-Wan said. "I know you can't fight now. But *I* could do it for you! I can hold back my anger and do what must be done. If Jemba were dead —"

"Nothing would change," Qui-Gon said wearily. "Obi-Wan, can't you see? Killing Jemba is not the answer. Jemba is but one Hutt. There are always more, just as evil and greedy as he is. If you kill him, it won't stop his plan from going forward. Another like him, perhaps someone worse, will take his place. What we must do is try to teach these people that —"

"But he is evil, isn't he?" Obi-Wan asked.

"What Jemba is trying to do is wrong," Qui-Gon answered carefully.

"I've never seen anyone who was so evil!" Obi-Wan burst out.

A sad smile touched Qui-Gon's lips. "And have you been so many places, young Obi-Wan?"

Obi-Wan fell silent. He had much to learn. His heart cried out that Jemba was evil, and that evil had spread to enslave innocent victims. If anyone deserved to meet a bitter fate, it was the Hutt. But he would listen to Qui-Gon.

"I've seen far worse," Qui-Gon continued. "If

you think of killing in anger, you must know such thoughts come from the dark side."

"Then how can we make him give the dactyl back?" Obi-Wan asked.

"You can't. You can't force people to be just and decent. Such qualities must arise from within — they cannot be forced from without. For now, I choose to wait. Perhaps Jemba will have a change of heart. Or perhaps some darker fate awaits him. In either case, killing is not the solution."

"But . . . you've killed before," Obi-Wan added hesitantly.

"I have," Qui-Gon admitted, "when there was no other choice. But when I kill, I only win a fight. It's a small, small victory. There are greater battles to be won — battles of the heart. Sometimes, with patience and reason and by setting a good example, I have won more than a fight — I have turned my adversary into a friend."

Obi-Wan considered this. Despite his pain and weakness, Qui-Gon was taking the time to explain his thoughts to Obi-Wan. Only yesterday, the Jedi most likely would have issued a stern order, then dismissed him. Something had changed between them.

"You're testing me, aren't you," Obi-Wan

guessed. "You've changed your mind. You are considering me for your Padawan." He tried to keep the eagerness out of his voice.

Qui-Gon shook his head. "No," he said firmly. "I'm *not* testing you, Obi-Wan. *Life* tests you! Every day it brings you new chances for triumph or defeat. And if you pass the test, it doesn't make you a Jedi. It makes you human."

Obi-Wan stepped back, as if Qui-Gon had slapped him. With a rush of emotion, he saw into his own heart. He had been fooling himself. He had told himself that he had accepted Qui-Gon's decision, that all he wanted was his respect. But somewhere deep inside, he had hoped that if he acted bravely and well on this mission, Qui-Gon would change his mind.

Now he saw the truth.

Qui-Gon saw the change in Obi-Wan's eyes. The boy finally understood that his decision was final. He should have been relieved. The boy's anger had left him. But something else was gone as well. Obi-Wan's hopes for the future had also faded.

Qui-Gon watched as Obi-Wan turned and wiped his face with his sleeve. Was the boy crying? Had he hurt him so deeply?

But when Obi-Wan turned back, only sweat was gone from his face. Qui-Gon could see no glistening sign of tears. Instead, he saw the worst kind of defeat.

It stung him. After all his noble talk of winning the hearts of enemies, he realized that he had just crushed the heart of a boy who only hoped to become his ally.

CHAPTER 17

Obi-Wan left Qui-Gon's cabin in a daze. He needed rest, but he could not seem to light anywhere. He tried his cabin, then the lounge. At last he wandered the halls aimlessly. He ended up near the engine rooms, staring out at the wasteland of the unnamed planet.

Five moons, in shades of red and blue, hung like ripe fruits out over a silent ocean. A flight of draigons hovered high in the air, asleep on the wing. The island shore was nothing more than a treacherous bit of wave-carved rock. Farther inland, dark volcanic peaks vented steam, and there draigons perched by the hundreds.

A door hissed open behind him. A moment later, Si Treemba stood by his side.

"We have been searching for you," he said.

"I needed to think," Obi-Wan answered. He was glad to see his friend. Si Treemba had showed him the greatest trust in the meeting with Jemba. It had forged their friendship, and they both knew it.

"May we ask what you are thinking about?" Si Treemba asked hesitantly.

"I thought that my time in the Temple was hard in many ways," Obi-Wan said. "The days were filled with study and effort. The very best was expected of us. I respected my teachers so much, and I thought I knew what I needed not only to survive, but to excel." Obi-Wan took a breath. "Now I see that I had no idea what kind of evil the universe could show me. I've never seen real greed before, not like the greed of the pirates or Jemba. It sickens me."

"As it should," Si Treemba agreed. "It is a horrible thing."

"And I am wondering . . . do I have the seeds of the same greed?" Obi-Wan wondered.

Si Treemba looked at his friend, puzzled. He saw great anguish on Obi-Wan's face. "Why would you ask that, Obi-Wan?"

"Because, all my life, I've wanted to be a Jedi. I craved it so much. I was willing to fight for the honor, and I became angry when others stood in my way."

"A Jedi gives much to his fellow men," Si Treemba answered thoughtfully. "He protects the weak, he battles for the common good. We do not think it is evil for you to want to do well. No, that is not greed."

Obi-Wan nodded, still looking out at the dark sea. He felt a deep longing to be home, back at the Temple, where things had clarity and purpose. Here, he felt lost.

"It will be light in a few hours. You have done so much for me already, Si Treemba. But will you help me one last time?"

"Of course we shall," Si Treemba said promptly. "But how?"

"Help me overcome my anger," Obi-Wan said. His fingers were curled into fists. He looked down at them and uncurled them, then gripped the frame of the view screen. "I feel such rage toward Jemba. He wants to use other people for his own gain, and I want to kill him for that. But I don't like the way I feel right now. Qui-Gon was right. If I tried to stop Jemba, I would be doing so only to satisfy my own rage."

"You seem calm," Si Treemba observed.

"Something has happened," Obi-Wan told him quietly. "I just realized something. Qui-Gon will never take me as a Padawan. He feels I am unworthy, and perhaps he is right. Maybe I wouldn't be good at it."

"And you are not angry?" Si Treemba asked, surprised.

"No," Obi-Wan said. "I feel strange, Si Treemba. It's as if a burden has been lifted from me. Perhaps I could be a good farmer. And to be good . . . to be a *good person* is more important than being a Jedi."

"But what about Jemba?" Si Treemba asked.

"Yoda once told me that there are trillions of people in the galaxy, and only a few thousand Jedi Knights. He said that we cannot try to right every wrong. All creatures must learn to stand for what is right, and not always rely upon the Jedi. Perhaps that is what the Arconans must do. I don't know about the future. But today I choose not to fight."

Obi-Wan turned to Si Treemba. "I asked you to leave your fellow Arconans to give us a chance to help you. I haven't gone back on that promise. I won't see you sicken again for lack of dactyl. I stand with you, Si Treemba. Somehow, we will find a way."

CHAPTER 18

Qui-Gon's Jedi healing techniques required him to put all of his energy toward knitting his torn muscles and fighting infection. Yet time and again he found his thoughts returning to Obi-Wan, to the look of defeat on the boy's face during their talk.

Why did the boy exert such a persistent tug? He had seen so many boys over the years. Time and again he had gently informed them that they did not have it in them to become a Jedi Knight. He had done it compassionately, and saved them from the difficult struggle of finding out too late. Hadn't he?

Resolutely, Qui-Gon settled himself on the sleep-couch. Regrets would keep him awake, and he needed sleep.

The ship was eerily quiet. Everyone was exhausted from the battle with the pirates. Qui-Gon heard nothing but the slap of waves on the shore and the soft rhythmic murmur of some animals skittering under the ship. He hoped the sound would lull him to sleep.

But he slept restlessly, due to pain or regret he could not say. Half-awake from a tortured dream, Qui-Gon rose and crossed for a towel to wipe his sweaty forehead. He drank some water, then rested his hot forehead against the cool transparisteel of his small portal. The craggy cliffs in the distance seemed to shimmer and vibrate. Was his fever getting worse? An odd, yellow mist blurred his vision.

He had risen too soon. Qui-Gon felt his way back to the sleep-couch. This time, he fell into a deep, dreamless sleep.

When he woke in the early morning, his right arm was stiff but better. A ship's droid had mended and cleaned his robes. As he donned them, he realized he was hungry. It was a good sign.

As he headed for the kitchen, he saw that the ship was abuzz. Arconans rushed past him, carrying crates of their personal belongings.

He asked one what was wrong.

"The tide is coming in," the Arconan said, "and it may swamp the ship. The engines are all down for repair, and we won't get them up in time. We have been ordered to evacuate."

"Evacuate?" Qui-Gon asked in surprise. With

the draigons outside, that sounded dangerous. "Evacuate to where?"

"Into the hills, higher up on the island. The ship's crew found some caves. We must reach them before the sun is in the sky and the draigons waken." The Arconan rushed away, heavy packs and boxes in tow.

From bad to worse, Qui-Gon realized. Shot down by pirates, wrecked on an alien world with Jemba holding a gun to them all. And now they would have to abandon ship, hide in caves with limited supplies. He could feel a rising danger. Perhaps the pirates would come to finish them off, or maybe they'd all starve, or die fighting one another. Perhaps the tides would rise so high that they'd flood the whole island.

The Arconans rushing past looked weary and battered. They had not gotten dactyl last night, and would have none this morning. Qui-Gon wondered how long they could keep going without it.

He strode to Clat'Ha's cabin and found her hurriedly packing her belongings. Her door was open.

She looked up when he entered the room. "You'd better hurry and pack," she said. "The tide is coming in fast and the sun will rise soon. We have to get off the ship." She grinned as she pushed a strand of red-brown hair out of her eyes. Her green eyes gleamed with mischief. "Jemba is furious. Maybe he's afraid he won't fit in a cave."

"Why is he so angry?" Qui-Gon asked curiously.

Clat'Ha shrugged. "Because it's something out of his control, I suppose. At first he thought the crew was lying. But even he had to realize we could drown if we stayed. It was almost worth it just to see him back down."

Qui-Gon frowned. "How soon do the Arconans need dactyl?"

The amusement in Clat'Ha's eyes instantly changed to worry. "Some of them are already beginning to fade," she said quietly. "If they don't get dactyl by tonight, they'll start to sicken and die."

"So soon," Qui-Gon murmured. Something nagged at him, an instinct telling him that he had overlooked something.

Jemba's anger. The soft tread of animals. A solid cliff that moved. A yellow haze . . .

But no animals lived on the island, only draigons. The crew had investigated for predators shortly after they'd landed. And the haze hadn't been in front of his eyes. A cave in the cliff itself had been glowing with a faint yellow light.

Realization sparked within him. "Tell the Arconans not to be afraid," he told Clat'Ha crisply. "I think I know where the dactyl is. I'll be back as soon as I can."

"I'll come with you," Clat'Ha offered instantly. "Or we could round up some help —"

Qui-Gon considered this. No doubt the dactyl would be guarded. But with hungry draigons hunting in the morning skies, too many people might attract their attention. Not to mention that Jemba would be on the watch. But one man dressed in dark robes, traveling alone . . .

"I'm sorry, Clat'Ha," he said. "I know you will hate what I'm about to ask you to do."

"I'll do anything," Clat'Ha declared fiercely. "We have to find that dactyl!"

"No, you don't understand," Qui-Gon said. "I'm asking you to wait."

Grelb the Hutt was good at following orders, especially when he knew that Jemba might eat his tail if he didn't. He sat on a rock midway up the cliffside, his blaster rifle at the ready. From here, he had a good view of the ship. Jemba had sent him here for two reasons — to protect the miners and Arconans as they evacuated the ship, and to make sure that no one climbed to reach the high caves.

Not that Jemba cared about the Arconans.

But now they were his property. He was protecting an investment.

So far, the draigons that hovered up so high in the air and that perched on craggy rocks in the hills had not spotted the Hutts and Arconans and Whiphids. The early morning mist shrouded them from view. Yet Grelb kept careful watch, prepared to shoot any draigon that swooped from the sky — or any Arconan that gave him trouble.

Last night, darkness had provided a cover for the hard climb upward into the cliffs with the dactyl. Jemba had ordered the Whiphids to do most of the work. Their feet were heavily padded, and would not make sounds while they loaded the dactyl onto packs and snuck away from the ship. No one had seen them, Grelb was sure. The rest of the miners on the ship had been busy licking their wounds after the pirate fight, and the Arconans were too afraid to stick their flat noses out of their cabins.

It had been a setback when the crew had ordered everyone off the ship and into the caves. Even Jemba had been worried that someone would stumble upon the cache of dactyl. It was lucky that they had forced the Whiphids to climb so high.

The mist was starting to break up, but gray

clouds were rolling in from the west. The air smelled of salt and distant lightning. Grelb worried that the lightning would drive more draigons to ground here on the island.

As the Arconans emptied from the huge dark ship, one man caught Grelb's eye: the Jedi Knight, Qui-Gon Jinn. He wore a cloak and hood, but Grelb instantly recognized him by his size and grace. Qui-Gon walked swiftly past the Arconans as though anxious to reach the caves. Yet it was not like him to hurry to safety.

Grelb fished a pair of macrobinoculars from his pocket and trained them on the Jedi. Qui-Gon climbed the hill quickly, without tiring. But instead of ducking into the first cave where the Arconans had already gathered, he continued to climb, inching along a narrow ledge in order to reach the side of the mountain without being seen.

Grelb would have gladly slithered after the Jedi and shot him, but dared not do so without Jemba's permission. He reached down to his comm unit and pushed a button. In seconds Jemba answered.

"The Jedi Knight is heading up the mountain," Grelb said.

"Where is he going?" Jemba barked. He sounded frightened, and for good reason.

"I don't know. But I don't like it," Grelb answered.

Jemba hesitated only a moment. "Take some reinforcements with you, and see that he doesn't return."

Si Treemba looked ill. The healthy greenish tone of his skin was fading to gray, and his small scales were beginning to flake off. Qui-Gon had been gone for hours now.

When Clat'Ha had told him that Qui-Gon had gone in search of the dactyl, frustration had filled Obi-Wan. He accepted that he would not be the Jedi's Padawan, but couldn't Qui-Gon ask him for help, just once?

Of course he had not. Of course he had gone alone.

In the dank cave, Obi-Wan studied his friend with a frown. The Hutts and Whiphids had taken the only lights into a larger cavern, so that only reflected light had worked its way in.

The Arconans had settled into the back of the farthest cavern — and what strange caverns they were. Each cave measured four meters wide at its narrowest point, and ten meters tall. Perhaps a dozen passages led to the surface. But tunnels opened wide into huge hollows in many places. Claw marks on the floors showed that an animal had dug them, yet the Arconans found nothing in the lair.

The Offworlders guarded the entrance to make certain no one fled. Stalactites hung overhead like glittering spears, and there was nothing to sit on but broken stones. In the dank shadows, the eyes of the Arconans glowed faintly.

Si Treemba was humming in Arconan. Others nearby did the same. Obi-Wan leaned closer to his friend.

"What are you humming?" he asked softly.

"We sing a song of thanksgiving," Si Treemba said. He translated for Obi-Wan.

"The sun is finally hidden,
and here our world is black.
In this cave we have the stones,
and our brothers at our back.

"Outside the storms may threaten
But here the day is calm.
We'll cleave to earth like flesh to bone.
With our brothers we belong."

It seemed a sad song to Obi-Wan. But he was not an Arconan. He was not used to making a cave his home. Perhaps to Si Treemba, the song sounded more joyous.

The Arconans sounded as if they were re-signed to their deaths. He could not understand such resignation. The urge to act, to fight, was becoming stronger by the minute. Obi-Wan struggled against the feeling. Hadn't he been warned about his impatience again and again? This was his test. He must live by the Jedi Code and wait, even while his friend faded. It was the hardest thing he'd ever done. But he trusted Qui-Gon.

"Promise me," Obi-Wan said quietly to Si Treemba, "that you won't let yourself die here."

"We won't let ourselves die," Si Treemba promised.

"Do you mean it? You'll hold on until Qui-Gon comes back?" Obi-Wan asked urgently.

"We will try to live, Obi-Wan," Si Treemba promised. "But the dactyl must come soon."

CHAPTER 19

Cautiously, Qui-Gon Jinn inched up a ledge that no Human should have been able to climb. In a pouring rain, he grasped small crevices with his fingers and toes, barely holding on.

He knew that he had to hurry. He had spent extra time approaching from the side of the mountain, knowing he would be too easy to spot if he climbed directly up. But at last he'd come to a point where he had to risk exposure. From now on, his path was straight up.

At the moment, he was more concerned about the draigons than the Hutts. The creatures were active now. Many had landed on crags above, as if to wait out the storm. He remained in the shadows, moving beneath rocks, afraid he might be spotted. Sometimes, he had to wait painful minutes until some draigon would turn its scaly silver head.

Patience, he told himself over and over again.

We must have patience. That was an unwritten part of the Jedi Code. Yet it *was* hard to be patient when so many lives hung in the balance.

His fingers were chafed and bleeding. Nearby, lightning split the sky and thunder snarled. The sky was dark and lowering. Wind gusted and whistled among the stones.

He felt terribly exposed. He was a big man, a big target for the draigons. A flash of lightning could expose his position — or even knock him to his death.

He stopped for a long moment, panting. Rain poured down his forehead and made his clothes feel heavy. He felt half-frozen, and still weak from the wounds the pirate had dealt. He glanced toward the ocean. Not far off, a gleaming draigon dropped like a blaster bolt toward the sea, its wings folded.

It plunged into the pounding surf, then flapped its wings. As it rose from the white-capped waves, a huge glittering fish wriggled in its mouth.

Thankfully, the draigon had not seen him. Or if it had, it did not care for Human flesh. Perhaps the draigons had never seen animals on land, and did not think to hunt there.

Qui-Gon did not dare look down. Up above him a few hundred meters, he could see a faint mist vented from a crevice blowing wildly in the wind. It would take the sharp eye of someone who knew what they were looking for, but the mist was definitely tainted with yellow.

The dactyl would be there.

The travel was hard. There were no trails. Not a rock on this planet had ever been crushed underfoot. If he stepped on a rock, it was likely to twist beneath him. Even if it didn't turn, they felt sharp and painful beneath his feet. The only plants he found were small gray lichens that crusted over everything. When they were dry, walking on them was like walking on carpet. But once the morning rains began to fall, the lichens turned slick.

Though he could feel the Force guiding him to the dactyl, it still seemed an almost impossible task.

Lightning sizzled through the air. Thunder shook the stone beneath his fingertips. Wind gusted at his back. Qui-Gon clung to the face of the rock wall. His shoulder throbbed.

Not much farther, he told himself.

There was a flash just above his head. Splinters of rock stung his cheek.

For half a moment, he thought that a lightning bolt had nearly pierced him. But he realized that it was too small.

A blaster. Someone had shot at him!

Qui-Gon craned his neck, and tried to look down. He spotted them immediately in the rocks below. It was difficult for a Hutt to hide. It was Grelb, Jemba's errand boy. He slithered along, flanked by several Whiphids. They raised heavy blaster rifles and fired again. The Hutt laughed merrily.

Blaster bolts exploded all around Qui-Gon.

His lightsaber was useless. There was nowhere to hide, no way to fight.

Painfully, Qui-Gon struggled upward.

Grelb the Hutt chortled in delight. His plan had worked perfectly. He knew Qui-Gon would have to appear around the side of the mountain and make the last ascent straight up to the dactyl. All he had to do was find a position, and wait.

At first, he'd been afraid of the draigons, and he'd kept still, hoping to be mistaken for a rock. But gradually, Grelb had grown comfortable. The draigons were probably fish-eaters, nothing more.

He didn't fear their teeth — but the rough stones of this world threatened to tear through even Grelb's thick hide. The Hutt wanted nothing more than to slither carefully back to the ship.

But right now he had a job to do: kill the Jedi. It was going to be a pleasure.

The Jedi was trapped on a cliff face above, squirming up toward the ledge where the dactyl was hidden. Qui-Gon had no blaster to shoot back with. He was a big target. It looked as if this would be an easy kill.

So Grelb told his cronies, "Take your time. Have some fun."

His Whiphids whimpered in delight. They loved to torment helpless creatures. They kept up a steady barrage of fire, purposely missing the Jedi with every shot. They hit just close enough to try to terrify the Jedi.

Grelb chortled, "Look at him squirm, boys! Reminds me of that puffer I ate for dinner last night!"

But the truth was, the Jedi did not squirm. He didn't cringe, or try to scramble away. His pace didn't change at all. Slowly, methodically, he climbed the cliff face, even as rock splintered millimeters from his face.

The Whiphids grew angry. "Is he blind?" one asked in a complaining tone. "This is no fun at all."

Grelb frowned. He did not want the Whiphids to complain. He needed their loyalty. "How about a bet?" he suggested. "See who can blow off his boot."

"Excellent!" the first Whiphid cried. "Bet you five I can knock off his boot in one shot!"

"In one shot?" his companion hooted. And the bet was on.

To sweeten the deal, Grelb bet against the Whiphid at two-to-one odds. Eagerly, he watched the Jedi make his steady progress up the cliff. The two Whiphids who made the bet brought their guns to rest on their shoulders. He waited breathlessly for the first Whiphid to take his shot. Lightning flashed, thunder roared.

There was a blast of wind at Grelb's back.

The Jedi had his right foot on a tiny ledge. He reached out for a handhold above. He was precariously balanced. One shot in the foot would probably bring him down.

"Shoot already!" Grelb shouted.

Behind him, there was a strange noise. Something like an *urp.*

Grelb turned to look at the Whiphid marksman, and there standing hugely at Grelb's back was a draigon. It had landed so silently, he had not heard it.

It was the first he'd seen up close. The draigon had tiny silver scales over all of its body, and huge yellow eyes like those on a fish. It had no front legs, only a single huge claw on each wing. And its mouth had the strangest teeth — like enormous needles that arced down from its gums. The monster vaguely reminded him of an Ithorian razor shark.

The huge reptile had half of the Whiphid marksman in its mouth.

"Aaagh!" Grelb screamed as he slithered toward the nearest crevice.

The Whiphids all turned and began to fire at the draigon.

Qui-Gon pulled himself up the last three meters, then wedged himself into the small cave. There, he paused, panting for a long moment, clutching his sore right arm. The acrid scent of sulfur and ammonia assaulted him. He peered farther inside the cave. The dactyl crystals had been thrown on the smooth floor of the cave, and were giving off the dull yellowish glow.

The blaster fire was coming as fast as ever. The guns made a steady *boom boom boom*. But the shots were no longer directed at him. Instead, the Whiphids had hidden in the rocks, firing at draigons. The blaster fire attracted them by the score, and draigons roared in the sky, flocking down from the cliffs. Several of the huge beasts had collapsed around the Whiphids, but others were wheeling from the skies in a feeding frenzy.

Qui-Gon looked down from the cliff, watching the struggle. He had traveled all morning without attracting the attention of a draigon. Now, by shooting their blasters, the stupid Whiphids were drawing them down in droves.

Draigons screamed, a great shrieking cry, and dove out of the clouds on leathery silver wings. They soared over the stones and swiveled their heads. Teeth gleamed under the strobe of lightning flashes.

The Whiphids scattered and tried to hide beneath huge slabs of stone. One Whiphid roared in terror as a draigon dropped from the sky and plucked it from its hiding place.

Qui-Gon used the diversion to load the dactyl into the cloth sack he had brought. For several minutes the Whiphids fought and screamed and died as dozens and dozens of the huge draigons plummeted toward them.

Suddenly, a great shadow blocked the light to the cave. A draigon shrieked, a cry so piercing that the rock around Qui-Gon trembled. He pressed himself against the side of the cave.

Outside the mouth of the fissure, the draigon clutched the rock with its wing talons. It let out the piercing cry again, and Qui-Gon knew it was no use.

He had been seen.

As draigons hurtled from the skies, Grelb slithered quietly away.

The huge hairy Whiphids danced among the rocks, shooting their blasters and bellowing war cries. They made quite a diversion.

Fortunately for Grelb, young Hutts — like certain kinds of worms and slugs — are adept at squeezing through tight holes and wedging themselves between rocks.

Thus Grelb moved quickly away from the huge Whiphids, and let them battle the draigons alone.

He was halfway down the mountain when he finally dared to stick his head up enough to gaze off toward the vast ocean. Even then, he held his heavy blaster rifle close to his chest. The tide had indeed risen, and now lapped against the hull of the *Monument*. But it looked as if Jemba had fled the ship in vain. It would not be swamped today. Grelb felt relieved to know that he might still make it off this rock alive.

Behind him, on the mountain, the Whiphids were issuing fewer war cries, and had quit firing their blasters. Grelb should have shivered in terror to think what had happened to them.

The draigon's shriek had alerted others from the flock. They vied for position as the first draigon wedged its long silver head into the cave opening. Lightning streaked through the sky behind it. Teeth longer than knives flashed near Qui-Gon's face, and he could smell the scent of dead fish on the draigon's breath.

Suddenly, in the middle of his desperation, Qui-Gon felt something odd — a faint ripple in the Force. As he concentrated, it grew stronger. Someone was calling him, a Jedi.

Obi-Wan needs me! he realized.

Astonished, he pressed himself farther back in the cave. He needed to be calm, to think. The boy shouldn't have been able to call him. Obi-Wan was not his Padawan. They were not connected.

But he had no time to wonder about the call's meaning. It was urgent and must be obeyed. Hearing movement, Qui-Gon quickly glanced toward the cave opening. For a moment the draigon beat its wings against the stones, blocking Qui-Gon's escape. Then suddenly it dropped from its clumsy perch.

Long had Qui-Gon followed the ways of the Force. Now he felt it beckon him. *Run,* it commanded. *Go to Obi-Wan.*

Qui-Gon's heart pounded. He ran three steps and leaped from the mouth of the cave, knowing that two hundred meters below, the sharp rocks stuck up like swords. Yet he trusted the Force.

He did not fall even a dozen meters. His leap carried him straight to a draigon!

He hit the beast's neck with a thud. The creature was wet and slimy. Qui-Gon almost slipped off, but clung to its scaly hide with the tips of his fingers. The sore muscles in his shoulder throbbed and burned. He managed to swing his legs up and over, so that he was riding squarely on the draigon's back.

The creature roared in terror. It had been flying up to eat the Jedi. Now it shook its neck, trying to throw him off. It shrieked again and again, then wheeled in panic and flapped its wings, dropping toward the sea.

Qui-Gon clutched his precious bag of dactyl in one hand and leaned close to his draigon's neck. Using all the power that he could muster, he whispered to the draigon. "Friend, help me. Take me down to the caves. Hurry!"

The draigons that were hunting Whiphids heard the desperate shriek of Qui-Gon's mount. They looked up and saw the man on its back. Now the draigons rose in a flock to give chase.

His mount flapped its wings and sped toward the caves. Qui-Gon wasn't sure if he could control the beast for long, for its small mind was cruel, and it was driven by a ravenous hunger.

Grelb had been lamenting the death of his Whiphid henchmen when he glanced back toward the mountain. Draigons flocked there by the hundreds.

To his amazement, he saw Qui-Gon Jinn leap from his crevasse onto the back of a hunting draigon. The Jedi wheeled away, down toward the ship.

Grelb's jaw dropped, and he dove for cover beneath a rock. There, he sat trembling. The Jedi was alive and heading back down the mountain. That meant only one thing.

Grelb was done for. Jemba would kill him with one blow as soon as he showed his face. Or perhaps he would kill him slowly, as a lesson.

He had not clawed his way to a position of power, second only to Jemba, to let a Jedi defeat him. He had worked so hard! All that killing, all that torture of innocents, all that profit, it could not go to waste.

He would have to kill the Jedi himself, before Qui-Gon reached the caves and Jemba saw him.

As fast as he could, Grelb slithered among the rocks.

CHAPTER 20

In the caves the Arconans were fading fast. Their bioluminescent eyes were growing dim, like fading embers from a fire.

Nearby, Clat'Ha and a couple of other Humans helped care for the failing Arconans. The usually fiery woman looked drained, worn out. There was really nothing they could do for the Arconans except make them comfortable.

Si Treemba hadn't stirred in hours. He whispered to Obi-Wan that he was saving his strength. Yet Obi-Wan guessed that his friend was really too weak to move.

Obi-Wan was desperate. He hated sitting by, unable to help, as his friend slowly died. A dozen times he had thought of running out to find Qui-Gon. But he resisted the urge. He had to stay by his friend's side and protect him.

Obi-Wan rested his forehead on his knees in despair. He stared at the cave floor. What was the use of all his Jedi training? He had never felt so helpless. Nothing he had learned, nothing even Yoda had told him, could have prepared him for this moment. He had come to the end of everything — faith, hope, belief in himself. He had failed. All his life, he would remember this, his darkest moment.

Darkest moment . . .

A memory stirred in Obi-Wan. He remembered a twilight conference with Yoda. "What is my limit, and how will I know when I find it?" Obi-Wan had asked. "And if I am pushed to the last, where can I turn for help?"

That was when Yoda had told him that in moments of extreme danger, when he had done everything he could, he could use the Force to call another Jedi. "Close, you must be," Yoda had said. "Connected."

Qui-Gon may not have thought they had a connection. But Obi-Wan had to try.

In the dark cave, he reached out for the Force. He felt it pulse, and he drew in its energy. He reached out with his Jedi senses, tried to feel the Jedi Master's presence. But Obi-Wan was a young man, and could not control the Force as he wanted. So silently, he simply called: *Qui-Gon! Come back now! The Arconans will die soon without the dactyl.*

From the mouth of the cavern, there was a

great rumbling laugh. Obi-Wan looked up. He had called Qui-Gon with everything he had, but instead, he had roused Jemba the Hutt. So much for his abilities.

Jemba towered above them, his immense bulk filling the mouth of the cavern. "How are you all feeling? Well, I hope," he taunted. "Well, in case you're not, I have dactyl for sale! Dactyl for the needy. All it will cost is your lives! We have some here, and much more hidden elsewhere."

All around the cave, Arconans began to moan. Some of them turned over and began to crawl painfully toward the Hutt with his offers of dactyl.

Disgust filled Obi-Wan. He leaped to his feet. "Stop this!" he shouted. Before he knew it, his lightsaber was out. He covered fifty meters of ground, leaping over dozens of poor Arconans, until he stood before the monstrous Hutt. He flashed the lightsaber overhead in a practice swing. The sluglike Hutt could be seen clearly in its light. A dozen other Hutts and Whiphids filled the tunnel behind him, but Jemba's bulk would make it difficult for them to shoot.

"Well, well," Jemba roared. "I'm glad to see that you are brave, even when your Master is not at your back!"

"Leave, Jemba," Obi-Wan managed to say.

He was choking on his anger, and because his voice was changing, it cracked comically.

At his back, Clat'Ha appeared, blaster drawn. "He's right. You're not welcome here."

"Very well," Jemba boomed. "If that's what you want, I'll gladly leave your friends to die."

"Leave them the dactyl!" Obi-Wan ordered. He gripped the lightsaber, could feel its heat warming the heavy handle. The blade thrummed in the air, and his every muscle ached to leap forward and begin slicing. Sweat poured down Obi-Wan's face, and he gritted his teeth.

"Isn't this amusing!" Jemba rumbled to his cohorts. "He is no Force user, this one. It's in the ship's records. He is nothing more than a farmer, a reject from the Jedi Temple."

Obi-Wan fought back his rage at Jemba's taunt. For long seconds he struggled as he sought within him for a place of calm, of peace. Then he remembered Qui-Gon's words. Jemba was not the true enemy. Anger was.

At last he found the calm he needed. He reached out with his senses to touch the Force. He felt it now, around him, in Jemba, in the stones, in the Arconans fading so fast behind him. He felt it and gave himself to it.

"Qui-Gon!" Obi-Wan shouted in surprise.

He'd been so focused on calling to the Jedi Master for help that he felt astonished to suddenly feel something else: Qui-Gon was calling to *him* for help.

"Jemba, get out of my way!" Obi-Wan said. "Qui-Gon is in danger!"

"Hah! Hah!" the great Hutt roared. He slapped his sides as if the laughing pained him. "Why does that not surprise me? Maybe it's because I sent my men to kill him!"

But it wasn't just Qui-Gon. Danger was coming to all of them. Qui-Gon wasn't just calling for his help. He was trying to warn Obi-Wan.

"I mean it, Jemba," Obi-Wan warned. "We're all in trouble!"

"What would you have of me, little one?" Jemba asked. "Do you want me to look down at my shoes so that you can stab me? Ho, ho, ho! That trick won't work on me. Hutts don't have feet!"

He was wasting time. Obi-Wan somersaulted once in the air, and landed in front of Jemba. Then, using the momentum of his landing, he sprang over the Hutt's head. Obi-Wan landed on Jemba's back, and the Hutt howled.

"You have been warned!" Obi-Wan shouted, gripping his lightsaber tightly. Then he raced down Jemba's tail and sprang over the heads of the surprised Whiphid guards.

One Whiphid fired his blaster at Obi-Wan's retreating form, but Obi-Wan managed to bring his lightsaber over his back and deflect the blow. He raced through the tunnels, past the startled Hutts and Whiphids. His need to find Qui-Gon was overpowering. He was astonished to feel the Jedi Knight's warning call, to feel this connection.

Behind him, a few Whiphids roared war cries, but Jemba shouted above the rest, "No! Leave him to me! The boy is mine!"

CHAPTER 21

"There, my friend," Qui-Gon said to the drai-gon. He pointed toward the caves. The dozen passages to the cavern were all set within a single hill, and from the sky the cave mouths looked like wormholes.

Qui-Gon fought to control the draigon's mind, bring it safely to the ground. He was worried. As far as the eye could see, draigons flocked toward the caves. Their roars were deafening as they called to each other.

Qui-Gon had seen the giant trees in the Silver Forest of Dreams on the planet Kubindi. Some of their vast leaves could be twenty meters wide, and when they fell in the autumn, they floated like giant rafts through the sky. That is what the draigons reminded him of. They dropped through leaden skies, just as the leaves floated from the Kubindi forests.

Yet these creatures were deadly; and like Qui-Gon, they were headed toward the caves.

Qui-Gon called with his mind, warning young Obi-Wan Kenobi again of the danger. Then he waited as the draigon wafted downward, close to the narrow ledge outside the caves. Qui-Gon chose his moment, then sprang off the back of the beast. He landed on the ledge, steadying himself with a hand against the outside wall of the cave. The draigon flew off with a soft confused cry, his mind released.

Qui-Gon had taken two steps toward the cave when he saw Obi-Wan race from its mouth, lightsaber held high.

Obi-Wan ran from the cave only to stop short. He stared up at the sky in horror.

At first, he'd thought it was just dark clouds. But now he realized that scores of draigons were blocking the sun. And they were all winging toward the caves.

Never in his young life had he imagined such terror. His legs went weak, and his mind was suddenly blank. He didn't know what to do.

Then he saw Qui-Gon heading toward him. Relief flooded him. The Jedi looked battered and bloody, and was holding one shoulder stiffly. Still, he was alive.

"Did you get the dactyl?" Obi-Wan called.

Qui-Gon nodded. "The Arconans?"

"Still alive, but barely. Go, Qui-Gon. I'll hold the mouth of the cave."

Obi-Wan expected Qui-Gon to argue, to send *him* back into the cave with the dactyl. The Jedi Knight merely gazed at him for a tenth of a second. In the Master's eyes, Obi-Wan saw respect and acceptance.

"I will return," Qui-Gon promised, and rushed into the caves.

In seconds, the draigons were on Obi-Wan. His lightsaber slashed and burned, sizzled and shrieked. Draigons roared in pain and fell before him. He was fighting better and stronger than he ever had, ever thought he could.

But he knew he could not hold the draigons off for long.

Qui-Gon raced through the caves, past Whiphid and Hutt guards, carrying his bag of dactyl.

Such was the look of purpose in his eyes that no one dared to stop him. Instead, Jemba's guards cowered in fear, until Qui-Gon, halfway through the tunnel, met Jemba himself.

"Halt!" the enormous Hutt ordered. "Where are you going?"

Qui-Gon stared evenly at Jemba. "You had

better get your guards to the mouths of the caves," Qui-Gon warned. "We're in trouble."

"Hah!" Jemba laughed. "Your foolish pupil already tried that trick!"

Suddenly a draigon roared near the mouth of one of the tunnels. The sound was astonishing. The cave trembled. Bits of dust shook loose from the roof.

"It has started," Qui-Gon said evenly.

He shouldered past the enormous Hutt and raced to get the dactyl to the Arconans.

Grelb squeezed between two flat rocks and lay for a moment, his heavy blaster in hand, staring down at the caves. He'd missed his chance to kill Qui-Gon Jinn. The big Jedi had already raced into the caves. But his pupil guarded the mouth of the cavern, lightsaber ready.

He wanted the Master, but the pupil would have to do for now.

Draigons hurtled from the sky by the dozens, converging on the lad. Even Grelb had to admire the young Jedi's skill. His lightsaber struck again and again, and the boy showed no sign of tiring. It was almost a pity to kill him.

Lightning split the sky. Rain pounded the stones over Grelb's head. One good thing about hiding under these rocks — at least it was dry.

He raised his blaster rifle and tried to aim at the young Jedi. The boy's lightsaber flashed among the draigons.

All I need now, Grelb thought, *is one brief moment to pull off my shot. Just one . . .*

CHAPTER 22

The battle was like none Obi-Wan had ever imagined. He felt no fear. He had accepted his death. The odds were just too great against him. Now he only fought to protect the Arconans. He felt no anger. He did not hate the hungry beasts that dropped endlessly from the blackened skies.

The Force was his ally.

He could feel it moving him, moving through him, and through the draigons. He leaped and somersaulted. He spun and slashed through muzzles and claws. The battle became a dance of sheer survival.

As he danced, Obi-Wan changed. He felt subtle promptings he'd never felt before. He saw attacks before they came. He sensed the flail of a tail before it happened. The muscles of the draigons seemed incredibly defined, so that he could read tiny flickers of movement that revealed which way a draigon would turn. Dead draigons piled on the ground around him. He gave himself entirely to the dance.

After several long minutes, he began backing toward the mouth of the cave. He had an idea. If he could kill the draigons at the very mouth of the cave, the bodies would block the entrance. If enough entrances were blocked, they might have a chance.

He fought his way back ferociously. He had just gained the entrance when he heard a familiar laugh.

"Well done, little one!" Jemba chortled. The enormous Hutt slithered from the shadows farther back in the cave. He held an oversized blaster rifle.

Obi-Wan barely had time to glance at the Hutt, for three draigons had gathered at the mouth of the cave.

"Help me!" Obi-Wan called to Jemba as he fought. It would be so easy for the Hutt to shoot the draigons. He could help with his plan. Obi-Wan knew he wouldn't care to save him, but Jemba would certainly want to save himself.

"Of course," Jemba chortled. "I'll help you — to death!" He raised his blaster and aimed.

Grelb huddled beneath his rock. Draigons lay at Obi-Wan Kenobi's feet. The boy stood with the mouth of the cave yawning wide behind him.

The Hutt chuckled softly. He saw his chance and squeezed the trigger on his blaster.

The bolt shot out — but to Grelb's surprise, young Obi-Wan must have sensed it coming, for he dodged to the side. The bolt barely missed him.

Grelb shouted in rage and prepared to fire again. This time, he would not miss. But suddenly, he felt huge teeth rip into his tail.

He had been concentrating too hard. He had forgotten to keep a lookout. A draigon had found him.

He barely had time to cry out before the draigon yanked him from under his rock.

Obi-Wan stood panting. He'd felt the Force, had dodged as a blaster bolt came from nowhere and sizzled past his head. Perhaps no one felt as surprised as Jemba the Hutt.

The enormous Hutt took the blaster bolt in the chest. For the briefest moment, Jemba stared down at his wound in disbelief. "Well, ha!" he laughed in horror.

His surprised eyes stared into Obi-Wan's for a moment. Thunder boomed and lightning flashed. Then Jemba slumped onto the muddy ground and died.

A draigon's cry wrenched Obi-Wan's attention back to his situation. He barely had time to thrust his lightsaber at the huge attacking mouth, then jump back.

"That was a little too close, I'd say," Qui-Gon remarked from behind him. His lightsaber powered up and glowed green. "I think you could use some help."

CHAPTER 23

Together, Obi-Wan Kenobi and Qui-Gon Jinn fought side by side. The Force pulsed between them. They knew without speaking where the other would move, when the other would strike. When Qui-Gon moved forward, Obi-Wan sprang back to protect his flank. When Obi-Wan leaped to the right, Qui-Gon made sure he was covered from the left.

Clat'Ha joined them, a blaster in each hand and a spare strapped to her leg. Qui-Gon and Clat'Ha had worked quickly to administer the dactyl to the Arconans, and they had revived enough to stand together and fight. Si Treemba and a group of Arconans handled any draigons who dared to breach the opening.

Obi-Wan's plan worked. Draigon bodies piled up at the entrance, blocking it. Obi-Wan, Qui-Gon, and Clat'Ha left a small squad to protect it and raced to the next cave opening. Then the battle began all over again.

Before his death, Jemba had ordered the Whiphids and Hutts of Offworld Corporation to defend the cave where they had gathered. He instructed them to fire from the rocks outside the cave. It was a foolish strategy. Hundreds of miners had been slain. Finally, Obi-Wan and Qui-Gon convinced them to fight at the cave entrance and use the draigon bodies as shields.

The Offworld miners and the Jedi worked to guard the cave entrances, but draigons dug new entrances through the rock, so that at times they broke through and came at the miners from above or behind. That's where the Arconans came in handy. By evening, it was evident to every Hutt and Whiphid on that rock that the Arconans were not cowards. They were creatures born to caves and to darkness, and when it came to time to fight in their own element, they proved themselves to be ferocious and cunning.

No draigon that tunneled through a cave's roof caught an Arconan by surprise. Indeed, the Arconans were so fierce that the Whiphids and Hutts finally retreated and left them to finish the battle.

Near nightfall Obi-Wan and Qui-Gon were still battling at the last entrance to the caves.

Smoke rose from the draigons' mouths as they let out their piercing cries in the dusky air. But the cries had changed from war cries to signals. Suddenly, what was left of the flock roared and leaped into the air. The draigons circled the island twice, then flew off in defeat.

When a ragged cheer went up from the surviving Hutts and Whiphids, Obi-Wan thought that it was merely a cheer of relief. But when a huge Whiphid came out of the cave and gave him a rough pat on the back, and when Hutts actually circled him and began to clap, Obi-Wan realized that these were not cheers of relief. Their former enemies cheered for the Jedi.

And later, when he and Qui-Gon went into Jemba's chamber of the cavern and took the rest of the dactyl back for the Arconans, no one tried to stop them.

Because of Jemba's orders, over three hundred Offworld miners were killed in the battle. Eighty-seven Arconans had lost their lives. The caves filled with the Arconans' hum of mourning.

Obi-Wan lingered at the cave, watching his friend grieve with his fellow Arconans. It was time for Si Treemba to be with his people. Obi-Wan put a hand on his shoulder and pressed gently, then walked away.

The miners' work force was nearly cut in half. While the Arconans grieved, Clat'Ha made plans for their future. She went to one of Jemba's chieftains, a Hutt named Aggaba, and said, "Aggaba, I want to hire you and your people."

"Which ones?" Aggaba asked suspiciously.

"All of you," she said. "You're temporarily the head of these men, until you reach Bandomeer. I'll buy out your contracts."

"And then what?" Aggaba asked. He had a cunning look in his eyes, as if he wondered how he might make a profit.

"I'll offer all of you an invitation to work for our mining company," Clat'Ha said. "We share the profits, so it's a step up for you. Think about it. When you get to Bandomeer, your bosses there will demote you, put someone else in over your head. This is your chance to escape from Offworld Mining, get decent jobs that will pay you better now, and in the long run."

Aggaba licked his lips and stared all around like a cornered Jawa. "Our contracts would not be cheap," he said. "I would want, say, two thousand per worker."

"Any money I give you," Clat'Ha countered, "would just go back to your corporate headquarters. So how about I make you a better offer. I'll give you twenty for each worker, and a personal bonus to you of twenty thousand just for signing with me."

Aggaba's eyes grew wide with delight. Clat'Ha hid her own glee. Aggaba would accept the deal out of greed. But the rest of the workers would have their freedom.

CHAPTER 24

Qui-Gon knew when to admit he had been wrong. He had underestimated Obi-Wan Kenobi.

The repairs were almost done. They were scheduled to leave at dawn. Qui-Gon left the ship to take a last look at the great sea. He needed a moment to consider all that had happened.

The surf pounded the rocks around him as he gazed at the planet's five multicolored moons, already beginning to dim with the rising light. He thought about Yoda's words, spoken only three days ago: "By chance alone we do not live our lives. If take an apprentice you will not, then, in time, perhaps fate will choose."

Qui-Gon still wasn't sure if fate had appointed Obi-Wan as his Padawan, or if it had just thrown them together for one odd adventure. He'd thought it a coincidence that both he and Obi-

Wan Kenobi were going to Bandomeer. After all, Yoda had sent the boy to Bandomeer, while Qui-Gon's orders came from the Senate — from the Supreme Chancellor himself! There was no way that Yoda and the Supreme Chancellor could have plotted this together.

But here it was.

Both of them were going to Bandomeer, and Qui-Gon had an uneasy feeling about this assignment.

And there was a further matter. It was not a simple thing for one Jedi to touch the mind of another. It was an intimate thing, the kind of thing usually done between the closest friends. Or between a Knight and his Padawan.

For the first time in a very long while, Qui-Gon didn't know what to do.

"When the path is unsure, better to wait, it is," Yoda had told him many times. Now he would use Yoda's advice, even though he suspected Yoda would want him to take the opposite position. He would not ask Obi-Wan to be his Padawan. He would wait.

And he would watch. They had separate missions on Bandomeer, but he would keep an eye on Obi-Wan. One mission was not enough to test the boy. There would be more to come. Only then would Qui-Gon be able to tell how true Obi-Wan was to his Jedi purpose. Bandomeer would test him, for Obi-Wan was unhappy with the mission he'd received.

Qui-Gon smiled. He had to admit, the boy was no farmer. He was meant for different things. But whether his path would intersect with Qui-Gon's, he still didn't know.

Until he did, he would not choose. The boy would have to be strong to dispel the shadow of the one who had come before. And Xanatos cast a long, deep shadow.

Qui-Gon turned away from the rocky shore and headed back to the ship. Yes, he would keep an eye on young Obi-Wan.

And besides, he had a feeling that fate would give him no other choice.

Qui-Gon walked through the labyrinth of the ship's corridors until he reached Obi-Wan's cabin. He knocked on the door.

"Come in," Obi-Wan called.

The boy was sitting cross-legged on the bed, staring out at the mountain crags.

"I'll be glad to leave this place," Obi-Wan said by way of greeting. "I saw too much death here."

"You did well," Qui-Gon said. "I felt the Force move in you."

"It was . . . astonishing," Obi-Wan said quietly. "I thought I understood its power. But I see that I had only glimpsed one corner of what it could do. For years, I thought myself worthy of it. But it was not until I recognized my own unworthiness that the power began to fill me." Obi-Wan turned to Qui-Gon. His eyes searched his face. "Do you know what I mean?"

Qui-Gon smiled. "You are learning. And yes, I know what you mean."

Silence grew between them, but it was a comfortable silence. Always before, Qui-Gon could almost hear the pleading Obi-Wan was holding back. Now he felt only acceptance of Qui-Gon's feelings, and his own fate. Another victory for the boy. He was impressed.

"We should reach our destination tomorrow," Qui-Gon remarked. "I fear there will be nasty business on Bandomeer."

Obi-Wan met his gaze. The look in his dark eyes was troubled. Yet underneath it, Qui-Gon sensed his strength.

"I know," Obi-Wan said. "I feel it, too."

Afterword

Obi-Wan Kenobi had been raised in the Jedi Temple at Coruscant, a world teeming with people, a world whose every piece of land was covered by skyscrapers.

When the *Monument* dropped through the atmosphere of Bandomeer, he marveled at the jungles and plains, the broad expanse of empty land and wide sea. He'd never imagined that there could be so much wilderness on one planet.

The port on Bandomeer was a small building, a hangar that could barely hold a freighter the size of the *Monument*. Obi-Wan followed Qui-Gon cautiously from the ship.

A planetary police officer was waiting. When he saw Qui-Gon, he hurried over. "Welcome. My offices will of course be at your disposal."

Qui-Gon nodded. "Can you tell me what this

is all about? The Supreme Chancellor said that you requested my help — mine specifically."

"Perhaps this will explain," the officer said.

He handed an envelope to Qui-Gon, who tore it open and pulled out a folded note. As he read, Qui-Gon's face paled, and his breath caught.

Obi-Wan read over Qui-Gon's shoulder. It said only, *I have been looking forward to this day*.

The note was signed by someone named *Xanatos*.

Meet the Guardians of the Force.

STAR WARS

JEDI APPRENTICE

The young Obi-Wan Kenobi.
The great Jedi Master,
Qui-Gon Jinn.

Experience their adventures across
the galaxy.

Read the all-new
Jedi Apprentice Series.

Jedi Apprentice #1: The Rising Force
by Dave Wolverton

Jedi Apprentice #2: The Dark Rival
by Jude Watson

Coming to bookstores this May.

SWJA1198